DONEGAL
FOLK
TALES

Ambassador Collins,

A small gift of appreciation
for all the support and
welcome from the Embassy
during my visit for
'Euro kids' last Nov.
Enjoy the stories,
Best wishes,
Joe Brennan
2013.

'I tell you that each and every one of these stories is true,' said the old fisherman. 'But if you are asking me if the events unfolded exactly as I have relayed, that is a different question. In fact that is a question, the answer to which is of little interest to me and even less useful to my life.'

Whispering Waves

A theatrical storytelling by Joe Brennan.

DONEGAL FOLK TALES

JOE BRENNAN

The
History
Press
Ireland

*To my parents Joe and Kathleen Brennan who fostered
my love of stories around the kitchen table. Also in
memory of Shiela Quigley, a wonderful storyteller,
inspiration, friend and true lady.*

First published 2013

The History Press Ireland
50 City Quay
Dublin 2
Ireland
www.thehistorypress.ie

© Joe Brennan, 2013

The right of Joe Brennan to be identified as the Author
of this work has been asserted in accordance with the
Copyrights, Designs and Patents Act 1988.

British Library Cataloguing in Publication Data.
A catalogue record for this book is available from the British Library.
ISBN 978 1 84588 767 4

Typesetting and origination by The History Press

CONTENTS

1

BALOR OF THE EVIL EYE

In the days of yore, a time far back out of the reach of chronology, there flourished three brothers, Gavida, MacSamhthainn and MacKineely, who lived in Tír Chonaill – the county we now know as Donegal – on lands looking over the fierce Atlantic. The first of the three, Gavida, was a distinguished smith who held his forge at Drumnatinné, in the parish of Rath-Finan. (The name was a reference to Gavida's forge as *Druim na Teine* translates from the Irish as 'ridge of fire'.)

MacKineely was the lord of the district, comprising the parishes of Rath-Finan and Tullaghobegley. He possessed a cow by the name of Glas Gavlin that was said to be so lactiferous that she was coveted by all his neighbours and many attempts were made to steal her. As a consequence MacKineely found it necessary to watch her constantly and keep her at his side at all times.

At this same remote period there was an island called Tory lying in the ocean opposite Drumnatinné, the home of the smith Gavida. Tory received its name from presenting a towering appearance from the continent of Tír Chonaill, and from the many prominent rocks towering into the heavens which are called *tors*. Here flourished a famous warrior called Balor, whose very name struck terror in the heart of the hearer.

He was a giant of a man who had one eye possessed of a terrible power.

The eye was a deadly weapon that had a foul and distorted glance and was kept covered at all times. When the lid was lifted it would emit its terrible beams and dyes of venom, like that of the Basilisk, and would strike any living creature dead. Legend had it that when Balor was young he was passing a house when he was attracted by the sound of chanting. Despite knowing that this was a forbidden place, as the magicians gathered there to work new spells, his curiosity got the better of him. He climbed up to a window high in the wall. At first he could see nothing but as his eye adjusted he saw the room was full of fumes and gases. As he poked his head further into the gloom the chanting grew louder and a strong plume of smoke hit Balor in the face. He was blinded by the poisonous fumes and could not open this one eye. He dropped to the ground where he writhed in pain. Before he could escape one of the magicians came out of the house.

The druid ran to Balor and realised what had happened. He was surprised that he wasn't dead. 'That was the spell of death and the fumes have brought the power of death to your eye,' the Druid said. 'If you look on anyone with that eye they will be petrified.' And that was how he got his terrible power and his name.

When among his own people the eye remained shut. But he would turn its deadly power on his enemies and they would drop dead. As he grew old it is said that the eyelid grew so heavy that he could not open it himself but needed help. An ivory ring was driven through the eyelid and ropes were attached to the ring to pull the eyelid open. It took ten men to lift it and release its murderous venom but in the process ten times that number were slain in a single glance. Hence to this day people call an evil, or overlooking eye, by the name of *Suil Bhaloir* – Balor's eye.

Despite this terrible power of self-defence it had been revealed to a Druid that Balor would be killed by his O, or grandson. Balor had only one child, a daughter, named Eithne, and he recognised that his destruction could only be brought about through her. So he shut her up in an impregnable tower, which he himself, or some of his ancestors, had built some time before. The tower was on the summit of Tormór, a lofty and almost inaccessible rock shooting into the blue sky, breaking the roaring waves and confronting the storms at the eastern extremity of the island.

Along with his daughter he imprisoned twelve matrons to take care of her. 'You must never allow any man near her or even give her any idea of the existence or nature of that sex,' he commanded.

The fair Eithne was imprisoned within the walls of that tower for many years and knew nothing else of the world except for the glimpses she caught through the window at the top of the tower of passing clouds and birds, and waves rolling on the sea pounding the cliffs below. The matrons tended to Eithne, making her life as comfortable as possible and tradition has it that she blossomed into great beauty. The matrons were ever on their guard not to mention the word 'man' or let slip any remote reference to that sex, for while they did not understand, or indeed agree with, the nature of Balor's command they followed it to the letter for fear of his wrath.

Despite all these precautions Eithne would still question the women about the manner in which she was brought into existence and of the nature of the beings that she occasionally glimpsed passing up and down the sea in currachs. She often related too her dreams of other beings, other places and other enjoyments which sported in her imagination. But the matrons stayed faithful to their trust and never offered a single word of explanation of the mysteries that enchanted her imagination.

In the meantime Balor, feeling secure in his existence regardless of the prediction of the Druid, continued his business of war and plunder. He performed many a deed of fame, captured many a vessel, subdued and cast in chains many an adventurous band of sea rovers and made many a descent upon the opposite continent, carrying with him to the island men and property. But despite all his victories his ambitions could not be satisfied until he should get possession of that most valuable cow, the Glas Gavlin. Therefore he directed all his powers of strength and stratagem towards this goal.

One day MacKineely, the chief of the land opposite Tory, and the owner of that prized cow Glas Gavlin, went to visit his brother's forge at Drumnatinné to have some swords made. He led the cow by the halter which he constantly held in his own hand by day and by which she was tied at night to keep her from scheming hands. When he arrived at the forge he entrusted her to the care of his other brother MacSamhthainn who was also there on business connected with war. 'Keep your hand fast on that halter for you know how precious she is to me and how many would love to take her away,' he said, 'while I go within to watch the shaping and steeling of my sword.'

'Do you take me for a fool brother?' he asked. 'I will protect her like my own.'

MacSamhthainn lay back against a tree enjoying the sun high in the sky while he was cooled by a breeze wafting off the sea. Balor, who was ever watchful of a chance to steal away the cow, saw an opportunity to fulfil his desire. He turned himself into a red-headed boy and made his way innocently to where MacSamhthainn lay resting with a firm grip on the cow.

'Are you getting a sword made too?' he asked.

'I am,' said MacSamhthainn, 'in my turn. When MacKineely comes out to guard the cow I'll go into Gavida and get my sword forged in steel.'

'That's what you think,' said the red-haired boy. 'I heard them talking in there at the furnace and they are using all your steel for their own swords to make heavier weapons and you'll have none.'

Of course that did the trick. MacSamhthainn jumped to his feet in rage and stuffed the halter into the red-haired boy's hands.

'Take hold of this my red-headed friend and you'll see how soon I'll change their minds.'

As soon as he turned his back, Balor turned himself into his own hideous self and, dragging the prized cow by the tail, hurried to the strand and into the sea, taking his ill-gotten gain safely back to his island fortress. The place where he dragged the cow into the sea became known as Port na Glaise or Harbour of the Glas or green cow to commemorate the deeds of that day.

When MacKineely's brother entered the forge ranting and raving he knew immediately that MacSamhthainn had been tricked. He raced outside to witness Balor dragging the Glas Gavlin behind him across the sea with great speed through the water. Within the shortest of times he watched the cow and man fade into a mere speck across the Sound of Tory.

It was MacKineely's turn to be angry now and he turned his rage on his brother. 'How could you be so stupid as to be tricked so easily?' he ranted. 'I gave her into your trust because I thought you had the sense to see such scantily concealed trickery.'

MacSamhthainn realised the error he had made and suffered a few boxes on the head from his brother without complaint, which probably helped avoid a major falling out among the brothers.

MacKineely wandered about for several hours distracted by his passions, and was not to be consoled in any way for his loss. But rant and rave as he might, the fact was that the cow was gone and it was a terrible blow. Eventually the brothers were able to persuade him to consider what could be done to recover the Glas. With his passions vented he went to see a Druid who lived in the area. 'You'll never recover the cow as long as Balor is living, for he will be ready with his deadly Basilisk eye and will petrify any man that should venture near her,' said the Druid.

MacKineely wasn't to be thwarted in his efforts to recover his cow so he went to Biroge of the Mountain, a Leanan-sidhe, who undertook to aid him in bringing about Balor's destruction.

She dressed him in the clothes of the women of the age and Biroge called up a powerful wind and wafted them both on the wings of the storm across the Sound of Tory to Tormor where Eithne was imprisoned. She knocked loudly on the door and demanded admittance.

'Help us! Please help us! My companion is a noble lady whom I've rescued from the cruel hands of a tyrant who had attempted to carry her off by force from the protection of her people,' said Biroge.

Despite Balor's wish not to admit strangers, the matrons did not want to refuse to help another woman in distress. They also sensed the great power in the hands of Biroge. They let her and her companion in.

As soon as they were inside the tower Biroge cast another spell and put all the matrons to sleep. MacKineely cast aside his woman's clothes and made his way to the top of the tower to find Eithne. He found her staring out at the stars with a sadness cast about her. She was the most beautiful woman he had ever laid eyes on. When she turned she beheld a figure that was familiar to her from her dreams and thought about in her imaginings all day long, a face that she loved dearly.

Declaring their love for each other they embraced with delight. They lay down together that night and when Biroge wafted MacKineely on an enchanted wind the next morning to Drumnatinné, Eithne was with child, the grandson of Balor.

Eithne was devastated the next day when MacKineely was gone and her grief wasn't helped by the fact that the maidens tried to convince her that all that had happened that night was a dream. Despite this fact they told her to mention nothing of it to Balor.

And so things continued until the day that Eithne gave birth to three sons. When Balor learned of the birth he was furious and filled with dread as he recalled the Druid's prophesy. He ordered that the three boys be taken from their mother and drowned.

Despite Eithne's pleadings, the three baby boys were snatched from her. They were wrapped in a sheet that was secured with a 'delg' or pin. Balor had ordered that they be cast into a certain whirlpool. As the bundle was been transported across the harbour to this deadly pool the delg fell out of the sheet and one of the babies fell into the water and disappeared beneath the waves. The other two were secured and cast into the intended pool as ordered by Balor. The harbour to this day is called Port-a-deilg or Harbour of the Pin.

Balor was delighted to hear that the children had drowned and the prediction of the Druid thwarted. But unknown to all, Biroge had been riding the winds that night and had seen the boy fall from the sheet. Instead of sinking to the bottom of the harbour, as was reported to Balor, the boy, the first born, was wafted secretly by Biroge across the Sound to the mainland. She brought the boy to her father, MacKineely, who sent him to be fostered by his brother Gavida, the great smith.

Balor quickly learned from his Druid that MacKineely was the man who had made the great effort to set the wheel of his destiny in motion. Balor made his way across the Sound, landing on that part of the continent called (from some more modern occupier) Ballyconnell with a band of his fierce associates. They seized upon MacKineely, dragged him to a large white rock and laid his head upon it. One of the band held his head there by the long hair while others held his hands and legs. Balor raised his ponderous sword high above MacKineely's neck and brought it down with a fearsome force that cut his head clean off with one blow. The blood flowed around him in warm floods and even penetrated the stone to its centre. The stone with its red veins still attests to the story and gives its name to the location of this deadly affair, Clogh-an-Neely*.

The boy was brought up in his uncle Gavida's trade which then ranked among the learned professions, and was deemed of so much importance that Brigit, the goddess of the poets, thought it not beneath her dignity to preside over the smith's also. The boy prospered at his uncle's side, growing to become an accomplished smith and gathering much wisdom from the furnace side. The great and good came from wide and far to engage his uncle and, as he worked diligently at the fire, the boy listened carefully to all that was discussed.

It was often he heard of the deeds of Balor who, believing he had baffled the fates by drowning the three baby boys, ventured forth onto the mainland carrying on his misdeeds without fear of opposition. Indeed he even employed Gavida to make all his weapons. He was unaware that the boy at the fire was MacKineely's heir, his own grandson, who had in him the power to slay Balor. He watched the lad grow into a fine strong young man and an excellent smith. Indeed Balor became greatly attached to him, ignorant of his power to have the will of the fates executed.

Now the son of MacKineely was well aware of the fate of his father at the hand of Balor and was acquainted with the story of his own birth and escape from destruction. He was often observed indulging in gloomy fits of despondency, frequently visiting the blood-stained stone, to return from it with a furrowed brow which nothing could smooth.

One day Balor came to the forge when Gavida was away on some private business so all the work on that day was to be executed by his young foster-son. In the course of the day Balor happened to mention with great pride his conquest of MacKineely. The furrows on the boy's brow deepened as Balor continued to boast about his killing and looting. Suddenly the boy grabbed a glowing rod from the furnace and thrust it through the basilisk eye of Balor and out through the other side of his head. In one swoop he had avenged his father, slain his grandfather and executed the decree of fate, which nothing could avert.

Some accounts claim that this took place at Knocknafola or Bloddyforeland but others, who place the death of Balor at

Drumnatinné, account for the name Knocknafola by making it the scene of a bloody battle between the Irish and the Danes. However, tradition errs as to the place of Balor's death, for it is recorded in the Mythological Cycle that he was killed by his grandson Lugh in the great battle of Moytura when the Tuatha de Danann defeated the Formorians, of whom Balor was a king. Lugh then became High King of Ireland.

*In 1794 the blood-stained stone was raised onto a pillar by Wyby More Olpherts, Esq. and his wife, who had collected all the traditions connected with Balor. Olpherts has committed to the durability of marble the name Clogh-an-Neely, but the Four Masters write it more correctly at the years 1284, 1554.

2

St Patrick in Donegal

Many of the High Kings of Ireland came from Tír Chonaill (Conal's country, Donegal today). One such man was King Laoghaire, who ruled at Tara when St Patrick brought his message of Christianity there. Now Laoghaire had three brothers living in the north-west of Ireland, one of whom was named Conal. When on Easter morning Patrick preached and converted many at Tara, Conal was there to hear him. So impressed by him was Conal that he extracted a promise from the saint to visit Tír Chonaill and to share his message with the people there.

Conal returned home and told all about this great man and said he could come to visit in the coming months. However, the months slipped into years and people paid little attention to Conal when he regaled on the subject of Patrick. It took several years before the promise was kept by St Patrick.

St Patrick was in County Leitrim where he had gone to raise to the ground Crom Cruaidh and his kin on Magh Sleachta, the Plain of Adoration. But the pagans in the area took a dim view of this treatment of their pagan idols. They stole Patrick's goat and then chased him out of the county to the River Drowes that bordered with Tír Chonaill. With nowhere to cross, St Patrick put his faith in the Lord and stepped into the river. To the amazement of his pursuers, the salmon of the river swam tight together and brought Patrick safely to the far bank. St Patrick blessed the River Drowes so that it would never want for a salmon either in summer or winter.

Patrick continued his task of driving the demons and snakes out of the land. After gathering up a small company of devils around Pettigo he drove them down a brimstone path and back to hell, that at the time led from a cave on the island in Lough Derg which is now called St Patrick's Purgatory and a place of pilgrimage. He travelled on through Barnesmore Gap, down the valley of the Finn, where he founded the church of Donoughmore (Donough is derived from Dominica – the Lord's Day; and wherever the name Donough or Donoughmore is met, it signifies a church founded by Patrick on a Sunday).

Patrick carried on to the parish of Clonleigh near Ballindrait where he met Conal. Conal was overjoyed to see Patrick and went to greet him warmly and with the respect in which he held him.

'Patrick you are welcome to the land of Conal,' he said. 'I am glad to see you. I have told my people about you and we have been eagerly waiting your arrival.'

'I'm honoured to reach you at last Conal and apologies for the length of time it has taken to get here,' said Patrick. 'But the land has been overrun with demons and devils and my attention has been drawn to many places.'

Conal then introduced Patrick to his two sons, Fergus and Conal (jnr). St Patrick ran forward to bless and salute Fergus, something which annoyed the younger Conal. Patrick could see that Conal felt slighted.

'Conal don't be offended by my actions. My reason for embracing Fergus first is because I see that a great saint will be born of Fergus' line. Thankfully this saint will complete the work I have begun here because I fear the challenge is too great for me in my late years.'

And so it was that Patrick had saluted Fergus in prophetic anticipation. In the years to come the prophecy came to be when Fergus became the grandfather of St Colmcille.

Patrick could see that the explanation of his actions had done little to placate the young Conal.

'Conal, hold out your shield in front of me,' he said in kindly.

Conal did as instructed and Patrick marked the shield with a cross.

'Conal, you and your kin will be greater defenders of the faith,' said St Patrick.

And so the shield of Tír Chonaill was struck.

Patrick then spent some time with Conal and his people. All were impressed by him and, unlike their kinsman King Laoghaire in Tara, they converted to Christianity. With his work done Patrick decided to push further north into the county to spread his message and drive the demons and serpents out of the land.

Patrick took a chariot and made his way to the crossing point at Tile Ford on the river Deale. Despite the flat flagstone crossing one wheel of his chariot caught on the riverbed and was damaged beyond repair. As he was near the far side he waded across to the bank to seek help from some men he could see working in a field. Now the men were deeply engaged in their work and were startled when Patrick approached. These people were suspicious of outsiders and knew nothing of this man.

'I am Patrick, a friend to Conal and the High King Laoghaire himself at Tara,' he said. 'Maybe you have heard of my work converting the land to the message of the Christian God?' With that he raised his arm to bless the work and the men in welcome.

Now the men knew nothing of what he spoke of and were uneasy in the presence of the stranger.

'Be on your way stranger, we have no need of anything,' said one of the men.

'But my chariot is stuck in the river and I need help to free it,' said Patrick.

'Why don't you go back to that lot on the other side of the river for your help?' asked the man.

With that Patrick flew into a rage.

'How dare you treat a man of God like this and not offer help,' he shouted. 'I won't pass over this river again and it falls to someone else to bring the message to you and save you from the demons of hell.'

The men picked up some stones and started to throw them at Patrick.

'And that village over there on the bend of the river will never amount to much and will never be more than a village,' Patrick prophesied before he turned and returned to Conal's people.

And so it was that that part of the county wasn't converted until St Colmcille began his work and even with the building of the bridge at Ballindrait it never thrived beyond a village.

Tyle Ford, however, remained an important crossing point. When the plantation begun Cavancor House was built as a military post to watch over the crossing point; its perfect view of it enabled the soldiers to watch the comings and goings.

3

THE BIRTH OF
ST COLMCILLE

Eithne, wife of the Chieftain Feidhlimí, knew that the child she was carrying was special. Now you might say that every mother thinks that but this was different. She couldn't say exactly what it was but she knew it.

Then one day as the birth drew close a holy man by the name of Fergna, who had been told by an angel that a holy child was soon to be born in Gartan, came to visit Eithne. When Fergna blessed Colm in the womb the baby put his thumb through the belly of his mother in a sign of welcome.

Eithne and Feidhlimí knew that their child would be a boy and had already decided that their son would not grow up to be a king, even though he would be a prince of Ulster. Instead they were going to give him as a gift to the Church to become a man of God. His name would be Colm, meaning 'dove'.

Like many people, Eithne was aware of the prophecy of St Mochta who had declared:

> A youth shall be born out of the north,
> With the rising of the nations;
> Erin shall be made fruitful by his flame,
> And Albain, friendly to him.

'When will this come to pass?' Mochta was asked.

'In a hundred years from now,' he declared.

She wondered if indeed the child she was carrying was that youth? A hundred years had indeed passed since that proclamation and Colm was due any day. In her heart she believed that it was him but she longed for a sign from heaven.

On the night before his birth Eithne was restless in her bed. She woke to a silent house but was startled by a vision of an angel, a fair youth.

'Don't be scared Eithne,' he said. 'Your son will be born tomorrow.'

Tears of joy trickled down her cheeks.

'In the morning go to the lake and there you will find a special flagstone floating on the surface,' he said. 'Take it to Rath Gno in Gartan for the birth. When your son is born lay him on the flag in the shape of a cross.'

With that the angel faded and Eithne went back to sleep.

In the morning Eithne told her husband about her vision. 'It was just a dream Eithne,' said Feidhlimí. 'A flagstone floating in the lake is just impossible.'

But Eithne was not to be deterred and she went to the lake with her servants where indeed she did find the flagstone floating. Her servants fell to their knees at the sight.

'Come,' she said, 'you must take it to Gartan. I must prepare for the baby. He will come this night.'

As the servants carried the flagstone back to the appointed spot Eithne came over weak and had to rest near a stream.

'Eithne,' cried Ludar Friel, a nephew, as he saw a drop of blood that had seeped from her and into the soil.

'I'm all right,' she said, 'but I must get back to Gartan.'

'I should cover this with some bracken,' Ludar said.

'There's no need; only you and your descendants will know where this spot is.'

To this day the clay is only collected and distributed by the descendants of Ludar Friel and must not be sought but given as a gift. The clay has healing and protective properties, protecting against the dangers of fire, drowning and sudden death. It also helps women who are in the pains of labour.

Colm was born that night, a cold clear night in December, and was laid upon the flagstone in the shape of a cross as told by the angel. There in front of all those in attendance the flagstone opened up, creating a place for Colm within. The shape of the cross has remained in the stone to this day and has been used for cures down the generations.

While all the attention was on the newborn and the miracle of the flagstone Eithne gave a short cry of pain. The woman attending her bent to help her and was amazed as Eithne brought forth a smooth round stone the colour of blood. The woman was terrified and cried out, attracting the others' attention.

'It has great healing powers,' Eithne said, 'and will give great succour to all.'

The stone was used extensively for healing until it disappeared in the middle of the seventeenth century.

On the same night in the Abbey of Monasterboice Abbot Buite, the founder, lay dying. With his last words the old man declared, 'Tonight a child shall be born, who will be glorious before God and men. Many years from now he will come to this place, and visit my grave. So he and I shall be friends in heaven and on earth.' And so it happened years later that Colm visited the grave of the abbot.

As was the custom of the day among royalty, Colm was fostered to Cruithneachán who lived in Kilmacrennan, with a view to being raised for the Church. There he dedicated himself to God. Colmcille's great power was shown one night when he was returning from a wake with his foster father Cruithneachán. Cruithneachán collapsed on the road. Not knowing what to do Colmcille starting praying loudly over the body. It was a still and calm night and Colmcille's voice carried to Cruithneachán's house where his daughters heard the prayers. They came running.

'He's dead,' one of the daughters said.

Colmcille was shocked by the news. Knowing that he had great powers one of the daughters begged, 'Please do something.'

Colmcille reached out and took Cruithneachán's hand in his and raised him from the dead. And thus began the legend of his healing powers and many people still turn to him today for succour, healing or protection, either at one of the many wells he blessed or using the clay of Gartan or Tory Island which is endowed with his special powers.

THE ORIGINS OF THE RIVER LENNON

Colmcille was visiting Ramelton when he noticed the emaciated bodies of the cows. They stood despondent in the field with each of their ribs protruding through their skin. There was a drought and the people couldn't spare what little water they had for their beasts.

'Don't fear,' said Colmcille, 'by the power invested in me I will bring water to you.'

With that Colmcille headed off in the direction of Gartan and took some of their worries with him. The people wondered what he was going to do. Was he going to draw water from somewhere and carry it back? When he didn't return that evening the people lost faith in him and renewed their worrying.

Colmcille had made his way back to Gartan where he knew there was plenty of water. He went to the edge of the lower lough and commanded the water to '*leanaim*' (the gaelige for 'follow me'). Colmcille started walking back in the direction of Ramelton and the water did indeed follow him. When he reached a hollow in the ground between Kilmacrennan and Milford he was tired and decided to rest. In a short time the tiredness overtook him and he fell asleep. How long he had slept he didn't know but the sun had dropped from the high of noon towards the western horizon. He looked about and was amazed. While he had slept the water had stopped at his feet but had continued to flow, forming a large lake which became known as Lough Fern.

Colmcille rose to his feet and once again commanded the water to '*Leanaim.*'

He walked on towards Ramelton with the water following behind him. The people of Ramelton were overjoyed when they woke the next day to discover a river running through their town which the cattle could drink from. From there the river entered into Lough Swilly, creating a small harbour, which years later was to become an important source of income.

And thus the River Lennon was formed as its name became anglicised later.

5

RATS ON TORY

You will meet many people in Donegal today, and indeed beyond, who carry a small memento, maybe on a key-ring, sometimes a small card. On this memento are two small spots of clay, one white, one black. Both are associated with the famous Donegal saint Colmcille. The white clay is from his birthplace at Gartan which will protect you from sudden death, drowning or fire. Many attest to its power in protecting people. Tradition has it that you have to be given this clay without asking for it for its protective powers to work. The black clay comes from Tory Island and is said to kill rats. Some people seek out the clay and put it in the foundations of a new house. This story tells of the origin of this tradition.

When St Colmcille was travelling the land converting the people to the Christian message he made his way across to Tory Island, off the north-west coast of Donegal. Now Tory was well known as the home of the fearsome Balor of the Evil Eye. He travelled there to preach to the people but also to find a remote place to live, as was the desire of monks like Colmcille. When he arrived he was made welcome but with a certain degree of suspicion. He lived among the people, sharing his beliefs and offering help to the locals with healing herbs when illness fell. In time the people of the island converted to his message and the island fell into its own routine.

Being an island, sitting on the edge of the wild Atlantic, life here is a constant battle. Storms roll in they turn the sea to a rolling mess. After a storm the people of the island would scour the shoreline to see if the sea had offered up any bounty. On one such occasion one of the islanders was out early searching the shore when he came upon the scattered remains of a ship. Nobody wanted to see a shipwreck but it did mean good fortune. He started to search over the wreckage when he suddenly saw three bodies lying amongst the remains. To his amazement the three were still alive, though barely.

'Help, help, help!' he shouted to his neighbours. 'Survivors on the shore!'

'Take them to Colmcille,' said one of the men. 'He'll know what to do.'

Colmcille administrated healing herbs and cared for the three until they had regained their strength.

The three had a come along way on their journey from Africa. They spent a lot of time with Colmcille who shared the Christian message with them and they were converted. The three lived happily among the people until the day Colmcille came to them, a shadow over his face.

'Brothers, it is time for you to depart from us and take the message of Christ to your own people,' said Colmcille.

'What is wrong?' asked one of the men.

'But we would like to stay here, if we are still welcome,' said another.

'You will always be welcome among the people but this is not your home,' said Colmcille. 'I'm entrusting you with the mission to take the message of Christ to your own people. That is what we must do if we truly believe.'

The people of Tory were sad to see their friends leave but helped prepare a boat for their long journey home. On a bright sunny day in July the people gathered to say goodbye to their friends.

'May you return safely to your home and may your people welcome you and the message of Christ,' Colmcille prayed over the boat as they set sail.

The people stood watching until the boat disappeared over the horizon, each sending their own prayer in its wake.

On the third night after they departed a huge storm rolled in off the wild Atlantic.

'Will they be safe?' the people wondered.

'Hopefully they will be well south and out of harm,' said the man who had found them.

'Pray that they will safe,' said Colmcille.

The storm raged for two days and two nights. On the third day the winds had died and the sea had calmed, and, as was their custom, the people headed for the shore to see if the sea had given them anything. There on the shore were the scattered remains of a ship. People began searching the wreckage with calls ringing out as someone found something of value.

But the cries died quickly when people began to recognise the goods scattered about.

'Oh no,' cried a woman. She was crouched over the body of a man. Tears ran down her face.

The people turned and recognised their friend who had left them only days before. In a short time all three bodies were found and this time there was no life present.

'Get Colmcille,' said the woman.

A young girl ran to bring him.

'We will give them a Christian burial here on the beach,' he said.

The bodies were prepared. The men began digging graves and the women keened over their departed friends. The three were buried that day with an air of great sadness.

The next day the island was shocked to learn that the three bodies had reappeared above the ground.

'What does this mean?' the people asked Colmcille.

'We'll bury them again.'

The next morning the bodies were again above ground. Now the islanders were very worried. They wondered if this was a sign from the old gods that they had turned their backs on. Some began to wonder about Colmcille. Colmcille was also concerned. He approached a man by the name of Doogan who had a field that looked out over the beach and the sea where the three had landed.

'Can we bury our three brothers in your field here?' he asked.

'It won't bring me any bad luck will it?' said Doogan.

'No,' said Colmcille. 'It may bring you blessings.'

Colmcille ordered the men to dig three graves in the field where their brothers could look out over the sea towards the lands they had come from. As the men worked Colmcille prayed over the ground and blessed it as is fitting for a Christian burial. But to the amazement of all gathered, black rats started to race from the open earth where the men were digging. Thousands, hundreds of thousands, raced out and ran down the hill, across the beach and into the sea where they drowned. Word spread across the island and all came to watch the unbelievable sight from the top of the hill. The bodies were placed in the blessed ground and all the people prayed over the graves. This time the bodies remained beneath the earth and from that day onwards no rats were ever found on Tory again.

On a visit to Tory some years ago a woman told me that a young lad who was working over in London decided to buy a rat and bring it back to the island to see what would happen. He had the rat in a covered cage. He arrived in Tory and all the bags were passed up onto the pier. When he went to check on the rat it was dead in its cage, dying as soon as it landed on Tory.

6

THE SILKIE SEAL

On the small island of Inishfree a short distance offshore from Burtonport, a fisherman named Padraig, lived alone in a small cottage. Each day he would take his small boat out to sea, wait patiently and see what gifts the ocean would offer him. When he returned he would push his boat high onto the shore away from the tide, gather his catch, tidy his nets and head home to his small cottage.

In the evenings he would often head to one of the other cottages on the island where the neighbours gathered to share the news of the day; they might even have news from the mainland if someone had been over. On such gatherings someone would sing a few songs and tell stories and invariably someone would tell a story about the silkie seal, a seal that takes off its skin to reveal a beautiful woman beneath.

Fishermen had great respect for seals for fear of harming a silkie. Of course some of them also secretly coveted the silkie. Why? Well, one reason was the beautiful woman hiding beneath the skin, but the silkie also knew the secret language of the sea. Knowing when the waves were whispering 'a storm is coming'. Knowing when the waves were whispering where to find the best fish. Precious information to any fisherman.

Now when anyone told the story of the silkie or sang a song to her mystery, Padraig would sit in the corner and grin.

'You're grinning Padraig,' said one of the older men.

'I can't believe you still believe in that nonsense,' said Padraig.

'You'll learn one of these days,' the old men chorused, shaking their heads.

One night Padraig was out fishing with a beautiful full moon hanging in the sky and it was perfectly calm. He lay on his back enjoying the gentle rocking of the boat and the waves lapping the side of his boat. The tugging on his nets disturbed him from his reverie and he pulled in a big haul of fish. When he got back onto the shore he went through his usual routine, pushing his boat high onto the shore out of the reach of the tide, tidying away his catch and his nets. He headed towards his cottage, his load heavy but his heart light.

As he made his way towards his cottage he heard singing, or maybe it was music, he wasn't quite sure what it was, drifting across the shore to him. There was no one on the island with such talent and he shook his head, putting it down to the late hour and his tiredness. But the sound tugged at him and soon he found his footsteps heading across the shore towards a small beach.

He crouched down behind an outcrop of rocks and glanced over to see three beautiful women dancing on the beach. He was enthralled by the graceful movements of the women and fell under the trance of the music. It seemed that the very motion of their bodies was making the music. How long he was there he didn't know but suddenly his trance was broken when the music stopped and the three women came towards the outcrop.

Hiding himself, Padraig watched as one by one the three women came towards the rock, pulled on a seal skin and disappeared beneath the waves. He couldn't believe his eyes.

Not only had he seen one silkie seal but he had seen three. He made his way to his cottage in a daze, not sure whether to believe his own eyes. He couldn't sleep that night as the three visions danced before him for the whole night. When the sun rose in the morning he went down to the shore where he had seen the silkies, hoping to see some evidence to confirm what he had seen but there was nothing.

That evening as usual he pushed his small boat out into the sea and made his way to his usual fishing ground. He threw out his nets and cast about his eyes hoping maybe to glimpse the movement of a seal. It was a quiet night for fishing and after several hours he pulled in his nets and made his way to the shore. Unknown to himself his ears were alert for the sound of that magical music that echoed within. When he came to the shore he jumped from his boat and pushed it high onto the beach, out of the reach of the tide. He stood listening to the wind but there was nothing on it but the sound of the waves. He gathered his nets and fish and made his way to his cottage. But his curiosity got the better of him. Leaving his nets and his small catch inside the door of his cottage he ran back to the shore in the hope of glimpsing the silkies again. He crept slowly towards the rocks and glanced over onto the beach.

'Ach, I should have known better,' he said. 'It was only a dream and I'm a bigger fool to think anything of it.'

Disappointed he made his way home the long way, sure to avoid the other cottages and any gathering of his neighbours.

After that night Padraig carried on the daily routine of his fishing. After a few nights of absence he returned to visiting his neighbours but whether they realised it or not, Padraig didn't laugh in jest when they told stories or sang songs of the silkie.

A month later Padraig was on the sea as usual with a beautiful full moon hanging in the sky; it was perfectly calm.

He lay on his back enjoying the gentle rocking of the boat and the waves lapping at its side. The tugging on his nets disturbed him from his reverie and he pulled in a big haul of fish. When he got back onto the shore he went through his usual routine, pushing his boat high onto the beach out of the reach of the tide, gathering his catch and tidying away his nets. He headed towards his cottage, his load heavy but his heart light. But as he walked he heard the sound of music or singing drifting towards him from the sea. His heart skipped a beat but he quickly tried to dampen his own spirit.

'I'm only imagining things now,' he said. 'I'm not going to make a fool of myself.'

But the music cast its spell on him and he found himself drifting across the shore. He crouched down behind the outcrop of rocks. He glanced over and there on the beach were the three beautiful women dancing under the full moon. The graceful movement of their bodies seemed to create the music.

Thinking quickly, Padraig reached an arm around the rock and stole one of the seal skins lying there. He ran to his cottage and hid the skin up in the thatch for safe keeping. He grabbed a blanket from the bed and ran back to watch the silkies dance. He didn't know how long he was watching before the three stopped their dance and the music died. One by one the seals ran to the rocks and one by one pulled on their seal skins. That is until the last one came.

'Wait,' she shouted to her sisters but it was too late; they had disappeared beneath the waves.

She searched frantically for her skin. Without it she couldn't return to her people beneath the waves. Suddenly Padraig stepped out from his hiding place.

'Have you seen a seal skin?' the woman said.

'A seal skin?' he said. 'No I haven't. Look where have you come from? Did you fall off a boat?'

The woman didn't answer and just looked out to sea.

'You'll get cold,' said Padraig. 'Wrap this blanket around you and come to my cottage; it's just a short distance away. It's warm and you can have something to eat.'

She had little choice and knew that her skin wouldn't be far from this man.

The silkie found a welcome at Padraig's cottage and knew that Padraig meant her no harm. She hoped that she would get her skin back soon and she could return to the sea. But the days turned to weeks and the weeks to months and before long to years. In that time she thought less about her sisters beneath the waves and love grew between her and Padraig. In time they had two children.

Padraig continued his routine of fishing every day. Sometimes his wife would warn him of a storm while other times she suggested a good place to fish. Life was good for both of them and they loved their children dearly. But occasionally Padraig would see her sitting looking longingly at the sea. He knew that a part of her still yearned to be beneath the waves with her own kind but they never spoke of it.

Now one night a terrible storm roared in off the Atlantic. Padraig and his family gathered in close to the fire, hoping and praying that they would be safe. The wind crashed against the windows, threatening to shatter the very glass. It tore at the thatch and Padraig feared that the wind would tear the roof from over their heads.

When the morning came the storm had calmed and Padraig went to see what damage had been done to their little cottage. He could see that the wind had torn the thatch away so he climbed onto the roof to repair it. The children played inside the cottage while their mother was busy with her chores. Suddenly something fell from the roof and landed between the children. The little girl lifted it and smelled it. She ran to her mother.

'Mammy, mammy, mammy, look what I found,' she cried. 'It's so soft and it smells like the sea.'

The mother's heart leaped in her breast. She took the skin from her daughter's hands and lifted it to her nose. It did smell like the sea even after all these years. As she held it she could feel the waves wrapping themselves around her.

'I lost this a long time ago,' she said. 'It's very precious to me. Now I have to go. When your father comes in tell him – well tell him I had to go home.'

She ran from the cottage and down to the shore.

When Padraig came into house a short time later the little girl came running. 'Daddy, daddy, daddy, I found it,' she cried. 'It fell from the roof and it smelled like the sea and it was so soft and mammy said it was very precious and she said to tell you she had to go home.'

'Oh no,' he cried and ran from the cottage.

As he came over the crest of the small hill he saw her making her way into the waves, back in her seal form. He called to her but whether the wind whipped his words away or she didn't want to look back she continued into the waves and disappeared.

Padraig sat on the shore staring at the spot where her head had sunk from sight. His heart was broken; a gulf as deep as the sea ran through its middle. He loved her dearly but he always knew that someday she would return to her own kind. But he did have the children to take care of and love. He lifted himself from the shore and made his way home, wondering how he was going to explain it all.

At night he would stand at his door listening intently for the hint of that magical music that the silkies made with the graceful movement of their bodies. Sometimes, especially when there was a full moon, he would make his way to the shore, hoping against hope.

Padraig continued his daily routine of pushing his boat out into the waves, pulling hard on the oars till he reached his fishing grounds, casting his nets and waiting for what gifts the sea had to offer. But now he often brought his children with him. And sometimes when they were on the sea a seal's head would appear beside the boat. Sometimes she would come to warn them that the waves were whispering 'a storm is coming'. Sometimes she would come to tell them where the best fish were to be found. And sometimes she came just to see her beautiful family. But they were never to see her in her human form again.

7

THE LEGEND OF RAITHLIN O'BYRNE

The tiny island of Raithlin O'Byrne is situated off the westernmost point of County Donegal. It is a low-lying grassy island indented all round with channels, bounded by cliffs and bisected by a sea arch. At one time it was a stronghold belonging to the chiefs of the Clan O'Byrne. They used it as their keep and the repository for the treasures and spoils of war.

On one occasion all the able-bodied men on the island were called away on military duty, with the island and its treasury left in the charge of only two individuals. One was the aged patriarch of the clan who was 80 years old and the other was his young grandson of only 16. The treasure was secreted away in a very secure place and it was felt that there was no need to leave a strong guard. The departure of the men was also managed very discretely so there was no apprehension of any hostile force paying a visit to the island during their brief absence.

The MacSweeneys of Arranmore, however, who had always borne a grudge towards the O'Byrnes, learnt by some means that Raithlin and all its treasures were left guarded by an old man and a young lad. They decided to take advantage of the situation and on a fine July evening put to sea. They arrived at

Glen Head about sunset and hid under the shadow of the land until it became dark. When darkness fell they rounded Ross Eoghan and steered cautiously for the island.

But the young O'Byrne was keen to prove himself and was keeping to his watch station with diligence. He spotted the hostile craft just as it doubled Ross Eoghan and realised that in less than twenty minutes the island, and worse still his dear grandfather, would fall into the hands of the ruthless invaders. He immediately left his station to warn his grandfather and to seek his counsel.

'Go straight to the port,' said his grandfather, 'and put your boat to sail for Dooran. Summon the McFadden clan, our faithful allies, to our relief.'

'But what about you?' asked the boy.

'Don't worry about me,' said the Patriarch. 'Even if the invaders put me to death by inches I shall not disclose the whereabouts of the treasury.'

'I can't leave you here to die.'

'Sure I'm already ripe for the grave lad and I've meditated on that certainty. It holds no terrors for me and if they slay me, as sure they will, I am prepared for the worst.'

'But …'

'No buts. They will be here soon; go quickly.'

Abandoning his grandfather was a terrible trial for the lad yet he knew there was no alternative but to follow his instructions. He hastily raised the sail and slipped the mooring. As his boat departed under the shadow of Ceann Ramhar he was spotted by his enemy as they approached Ceann Caol.

The wind was favourable to the lad and within three hours he anchored at Dooran. He ran immediately to summon the McFadden clan and inform them of the situation of things on Raithlin and the danger his poor grandfather was in.

The McFaddens began to deliberate how they could best react to the emergency.

'It's impossible to reach Raithlin before daylight arrives,' said one.

'There's no way we can approach the island in daylight,' said another. 'You know how difficult it is to land there. They'll easily spot us and stop us from landing.'

They each fell to deliberating in their own minds but the silence was broken by an aged matron who offered her wise counsel.

'If you start now,' she said, 'you will be off Carrigan Head about sunrise. The MacSweeneys cannot observe you of course till you round the Carrigan. Don't pass Carrigan till after sunrise. You know that the sky these days is beautifully clear so no clouds will dim the rising sun or stop its beams dancing on the face of the waters. After passing the Carrigan, when you come in view of Raithlin, be sure to steer your boat so that it is always in a line between the sun and the island. Then their sentinel won't notice your approach as you will be in the track where the sunbeams play upon the waters and his eyes will be dazzled when he looks on the 'gath-gréine – the golden rays of the sun – in which your boat can quietly sail along.'

A great applause rang out from the assembly as they told her how much they appreciated her good counsel. So the clan readied the boats and set sail to Raithlin. When they were off Muckross the day began to dawn and when they were nearing Carrigan Head the sun appeared over the tops of the distant mountains of Barnesmore. The captain kept the boat in the line of the solar beams, just as the old matron had advised, and they succeeded in reaching the port eluding the vigilance of the watchman.

And all the while that the faithful youth was summoning the McFadden clan, events on Raithlin had also been unfolding through the night. You will recall that the MacSweeneys had observed O'Byrne's boat passing away under Ceann Ramhar, just as they were coming up at Ceann Caol. However, they did not pursue it as they were more intent on securing the treasure on the island. On landing they seized the old chieftain, made him a prisoner and demanded to be conducted to where the treasure lay. But they quickly realised that despite his eighty years they were dealing with a man possessed with a stubborn resolve.

They threatened to kill him if he did not obey their orders but it was of no use.

They promised him his liberty if he complied; it was equally in vain.

They reasoned, they blustered, they coaxed and they threatened but all to no avail.

The old man was fixed in his determination not to give them the least intimation where the treasure lay hidden. As a last resort they started torturing him in various ways in the futile hope of ever getting at the hidden treasures. One of their number however, more kindly than the rest, protested against the cruel tortures.

'This is cowardly and is even more disgraceful for being practised upon this helpless old man,' he said.

But his protests fell on deaf ears, so he withdrew from the company that he might not witness the cruel tortures or be seen to approve by his presence. He retired to a rock at Ceann Ramhar, far down the face of the cliff, where he occupied himself in watching the brilliant blaze of the morning sun, as herald-like it mounted the deep blue sky and gave notice to the starry host to retire before the great ruler of the day.

At frequent intervals one of the party of the MacSweeneys would go to the bank of the sea and carefully scan the horizon to see if any hostile sail was coming. But the report was always

in the negative as the McFaddens stuck to the course determined by the wise matron.

The MacSweeneys were totally startled by the tramp of
feet rushing towards them. They all sprang to the spot where
they had left their weapons but it was too late. Stunned by the
sudden attack, they scarcely knew what had happened until
they were slaughtered indiscriminately where they stood.
Only one man was spared in order to bring him as a captive
to grace their triumph and furnish evidence of their victory.

'I can take you to another of my kin who sits below on a rock
at the base of the cliff,' said the captured MacSweeney, trying
to ingratiate himself with his captors. He was the one who had
removed himself from the torturing of the old man and was out
of doors when they were overpowered.

The traitorous captive was placed in the fore-part of the
boat. On nearing the rock on which sat the fugitive he raised
a heavy spar with the intention of dispatching his fellow clans-
man. The MacFaddens, however, saved the poor fellow from
the traitor's murderous designs. They took him into their boat
as a prisoner and his cowardly would-be murderer they
later hanged for his treason to his clan. Thus showing in
what high regard loyalty to one's clan was held.

The old man required immediate attention. His
tortures were so great that it was clear that he wasn't
long for this world. They decided to remove him to
Malinbeg on the mainland where he would have
the consolations of religion administered and
spend his last moments soothed by friends. He
was placed in the boat that the MacFaddens
had come by, in which a few dear friends were
waiting to bring him ashore. The remainder,
including their new captive, embarked in the boat

the MacSweeneys had brought to the island. The boat carrying the old chief shot ahead of the other.

'Well look at that,' said one of the MacFadden clan. 'Even in the speed of your boats you're inferior to us.'

'If you let me take the helm I'll show you what a Ross's boat can do,' he said. 'The MacFaddens don't know how to steer.'

Piqued at his taunt, the clansmen accepted his offering. On the pretence of taking the inside line of the other boat when rounding a projection, he took the opportunity to deflect his own course so as to run her upon the rock. The MacFaddens instantly detected his mischievous purpose and with swift action saved themselves from destruction. The baffled steersman was left lamenting aloud that he had lost a fine opportunity of avenging the fate of his fallen clansmen. His speech was applauded by the MacFaddens, for they admired in every man an heroic devotion to his own tribe, and when they reached Malinbeg they freely gave him his liberty.

After getting ashore the old chieftain lingered a day or two in great agony and at last passed quietly out of this and into the next world at peace. Death indeed had no terrors for him, for he was long awaiting it. And when at last it arrived he was fully prepared.

8

ARRANMORE SEAL STORY

Like fishermen along the coast of Ireland, and on across to
Scotland, the men of Arranmore Island off the west coast
of Donegal do not harm the seals that inhabit their waters.
Some believe that the seals are an enchanted race. Others
believe they are humans who have been metamorphosed by
their own witchcraft.

One such fisherman was a man by the name of Rodgers.
One day some of his nets had broken loose and had washed
into the cave. He manoeuvred his small skiff through the
mouth of the cave and was enraged when he saw a seal eating
the fish that were caught in his nets. He jumped up in his skiff
and swung a club at the seal's head without thinking. The seal
disappeared beneath the water and was gone. Gathering his
wits he called into the water that he was sorry, fully aware of
what he had done.

For some time after he thought about the seal and wondered
if it would bode ill for him. But nothing bad came to him and
the event drifted from his mind. Then one night, when he was
out in his skiff, a huge storm roared in off the Atlantic. His
small skiff was lifted up by the waves and battered about for
the hours of darkness. On several occasions Rodgers felt he

was going to be swallowed by the sea and that he would never see home again. But when the sun brightened the sky, the seas became calm and his small skiff was washed up safely onto the shore. Rodgers had no idea where he was and so approached a small house not far from the shore.

'Hello,' he said at the door.

'Enter young Rodgers,' said the voice inside.

He was amazed to be addressed by his name in what he took to be a strange land. His surprise was even greater when he learned that he had been washed all the way to Scotland.

'And how is it that you know who I am?' asked Rodgers. 'My people and I have never travelled to these shores before and I don't recognise you from the island.' (Of course in these days people travelled back and forward to Scotland for 'tatty hoking' each year.)

The man pulled back the cap on his head to reveal a large scar on his temple.

'Ah, it was yourself that gave me this scar,' said the man.

Rodgers looked incredulous.

'But I have never laid a hand on any man,' said Rodgers.

'Don't you remember that day in the cave when I was eating your fish?' said the man.

'But, but … I did say I was sorry,' said Rodgers.

The old man could see fear in Rodgers eyes.

'I do not blame you Rodgers, for you were not aware of what you were doing and only protecting your livelihood,' said the old man.

Rodgers returned safely to his home on Arranmore and never again did anything to harm a seal. Whenever anyone said a bad word about the seal folk he would defend them and the respect that people showed for them.

9

THE EAGLE'S NEST

The majestic cliffs of Sliabh Liag, meaning the mountain of flags reflecting the rock structure laid bare by the waves, are more commonly referred to these days by the anglicised version Slieve League. They are among the highest sea cliffs in Europe and tower above the ocean waves on the west coast of Donegal. On a calm day the waves wash gently at the foot of the cliffs while the cliffs stand strong against the thunderous storm waves that the great Atlantic flings at the coast. These majestic cliffs have attracted visitors right through the ages, some to contemplate their beauty, others to marvel at their strength and power.

Many moons ago a king was out on the cliffs admiring their beauty and strength. He wanted to think that his own rule mirrored that of the cliffs; a steady strength to hold back the waves of attack from the sea of enemies around him; beauty and majesty to rule his people with fairness.

As he and his retinue made their way along the cliff tops they saw a huge eagle flying high above their heads. The king kept a keen eye on the eagle as it glided high on the air currents, carefree and untroubled. His own mind was troubled greatly of late. Not by the intrigue of rule or the threat of attack from other clans. No, his troubles were of a more domestic nature.

Despite being married for ten years he and his wife had yet to conceive a child. They had consulted all the wise ones to see if they could help. All had soothing words to offer and various suggestions of herbal concoctions, prayers and midnight rituals. And yet no child had come to them. The night before, the queen had woken from a nightmare. She was inconsolable and could hardly tell him what had shaken her.

'I dreamed that we had a child, a beautiful little boy. It was a beautiful sunny day and the child was lying in his swaddle of blankets outside in the sun. The maid was sitting with him. I needed the maid to help me and I told her to leave the child in the sun,' she explained. 'I came back out with the maid and a terrible thing happened.'

Tears leapt to her eyes and she became distraught again. Through her tears she continued her story. 'A huge eagle swooped down and grabbed the child between its claws. We ran shouting at the bird but it was not bothered in the least. It flapped its wings and took to the air as if the child was a mere twig,' she said. 'I lost him. After waiting so long, I lost him.'

'It's only a dream my love,' the king tried to soothe her. 'It's only a dream.'

A dream. That's how he felt about having a child, an heir; a dream. But it wasn't a dream, it was a nightmare. A living nightmare. He had watched his wife grow more distant and vacant as the years passed.

Coming up onto the cliffs gave him a welcome break from the gloom that had settled over his home. He watched the eagle up high without its worries, trusting the wind to carry him wherever he needed to go. He had heard stories about eagles taking small children. It was nonsense and he knew it, but try as he might he couldn't convince his people of this. Some people even went so far as to kill these majestic birds, which enraged him.

He moved on up the cliffs. With his mind preoccupied as it was, he thought he heard the cry of a child. He glanced around wondering if there were others on the cliff but there was no one. He smiled to himself, aware that his longing was taking hold of him.

'Did you hear that?' called one of his servants.

'What?' said the king.

'It's a child crying,' he said.

'Och, you're imagining it,' said one of the others. 'It's just the wind.'

The king raised his hand to bring them to a stop and they listened. They could hear the waves washing the feet of the cliffs, they could hear the breeze sweeping past them, they could hear the cry of the eagle and then in amongst it all was the cry of a child.

'Spread out and search for it,' the king commanded.

They looked everywhere, behind and under every rock, and down every rabbit hole. The king himself wandered to the edge of the cliffs to watch the soothing waves. What he saw below him stunned him. A short distance down was a protruding ledge and on it there was an eagle's nest. And lying in the nest was a small baby crying out.

'Over here,' the king called.

They all stood in amazement at the sight. Some began to wonder who was going to climb down and stepped back from the edge as fear gripped them.

'We have to rescue it,' said the king. 'I'll climb down.'

'You can't do that,' said his attendant.

'It's too dangerous. You could fall easily,' said another.

'You don't understand,' said the king. 'This is a gift for the queen and I.' He didn't want to explain about his wife's dream but they seemed to understand.

'But if you fall he will have no father and we'll have no king,' said his attendant.

The king knew this but felt it was his duty. 'I insist,' he said. 'Gather up whatever you can to make a support to hold me.'

The servants gathered up all of the materials they had and fashioned a rope to hold their king. Before stepping over the edge, the king glanced into sky to see where the eagle was but it was nowhere to be seen. The king began the descent, moving slowly and carefully. While the nest was only a short distance below it took him some time to reach it. As he climbed he was aware of the waves way below him.

When he reached the nest he found a small baby boy wearing purple clothes and gold bangles on his arms. The king took the boy in his arms with great care and made him safe. With the help of his servants he made it safely to the top of the cliff.

When the king returned there was great excitement but he was quick to dampen the mood as he knew there was a mother and father, mostly likely another king and queen, who had lost their child. Messengers were sent out to seek these parents but they all returned without finding them. It was decided then that they would raise the boy as their own and great celebrations erupted. The queen was overjoyed and thanked the heavens for her great gift. However, she was always careful not to leave him unattended out of doors until he had grown beyond the reach of eagles.

Now at that time there was a man by the name of Andrew MacIntyre who resided in Croughlin, not far from Bunglas, who during the famine came upon an eagle's nest on the cliffs with two eaglets in it and found the leftovers of their meals scattered about. He retrieved these to feed his own family. With a full stomach he could see that here was a possible solution to his travails. He went back to the nest and tied the beaks of the chicks. Now when the mother brought a rabbit or lamb the chicks couldn't tear into the flesh. The man would return and take the food. But he was always careful to feed the chicks something. He couldn't afford to let them starve as his food supply would dry up.

Whether it was the way of things because of the famine or something else, the man found human parts in the nest and on one occasion a baby. He was horrified. Soon the only food that the eagle was bringing to the nest was human in nature. Outraged he decided to put an end to this and set fire to the nest and the chicks.

Now in that same village of Croughlin there lived a man named McGlinchey with his wife and their only child called Brighid, who was 2½ years old at the time of this story. One fine day in summer little Brighid was outside playing with a girl who was a little older than her while the mother was inside, cheerfully humming along to the music of her spinning wheel.

Suddenly the older girl rushed into the cottage in a state of great distress and announced that a big bird was trying to carry Brighid away. Terror-stricken, the mother leapt to her feet and rushed outside. But it was too late as the bird had already taken to the air and was climbing high over the hills, taking Brighid with him.

The cries of the mother had drawn her neighbours to her side and they watched as little Brighid struggled to free herself from the grasp of the piercing talons. Her cries of 'mama' drifted to their ears and brought tears to many an eye. Horrorified they watched the eagle fly over the steep hill, carrying the child.

The eagle flew on to the coast and then out over the cliffs and on over the briny waves in the direction of Connaught. The gathered crowd moved towards the cliff until they stood on a lofty eminence overlooking the sea, not far from Carrigan Head, watching the fading speck of the bird over the sea.

Then an old man arrived on the scene and startled the bewildered assembly when he said, 'Cease your silly gazing. What can we, or any human being, do to stop the wild bird of the mountain? There is only one power that can control him – the power of God.'

They fell to their knees and prayed fervently to the Lord for the safe return of the child. They beseeched the Lord to exert His Almighty power and show forth His tender mercy.

All eyes were fixed on the horizon but only the sharp eyes of the young could still discern the tiny speck that was the bird carrying away the child. Suddenly a youngster shouted that he thought the speck was becoming somewhat larger. Three or four voices soon corroborated this. Soon it was clear to all to see that the eagle had been moved to return to the cliffs. Their prayers continued until they could see clearly that the little girl was still struggling in the grasp of the eagle. On that they rushed in the direction of the eyrie so as to snatch away the dear little victim.

The eagle alighted on Carrigan Head but quickly took to the air again in the direction of Malinbeg, by now relieved of its burden. The delighted mother, who on the approach of the eagle was led by her motherly instincts to the place where the eagle landed, was the first to reach her beloved child who was lying on the green grass at the edge of the cliff, calling lustily 'mama'. The assembly then fell to their knees and thanked God for His tender mercy and for moving His power for the preservation of the child. The little girl stood up as her mother approached and complained that the naughty bird had made holes in her side. On examination it was found that both sides of her chest were badly lacerated from the tight grip of the bird. In later years Brighid, who married and lived for nearly a hundred years, would sometimes verify the story by exhibiting the wounds sustained from the eagle's talons.

Now one man who had listened to the stories, and observed this event, cobbled together a plan to deal with a problem of his own. Like the king, he and his wife were without child. The two were devastated by this and the man was desperate to find a way to relieve the pain. The man had an affair with another woman in a neighbouring village and she fell pregnant. When the child was born the mother nursed him for some months till the boy was strong and healthy. The man then took the boy home and claimed that he had discovered the baby boy abandoned in the eagle's nest.

'It's the answer to our prayers,' he told his wife.

She was a little sceptical but her husband pointed to the stories and events surrounding the taking and return of little Brighid. The man and woman reared the child as if he was their own and the true mother never whispered a word of her involvement.

10

THE GLENTIES
MIDWIFE

There was an old widow woman who lived a short distance from the village of Glenties. She went about her business with a heavy heart and a bend in her back that told of great sadness. The weight that she carried on her shoulders was grief. When her only daughter was on the cusp of womanhood she suddenly died. Her loss broke the woman's heart. She tried to put a brave face on her loss but tears were never far from her eyes when she pictured her beautiful daughter.

One day as she was leaving the village on a fair day she was accosted by a man she didn't recognise.

'Excuse me ma'am, but my young wife is about to give birth to our first child and she needs assistance,' said the man.

'Oh, I'm not the woman for that,' she said. In her heart she knew she couldn't bear to witness the joy of a birth.

'Please,' the man said. 'The child will be here soon and my wife needs assistance. It's her first.'

'Find someone else,' she said. She turned to hurry on her way but the man gripped her arm. He wasn't hurting her but there was a firmness in his grip that commanded her attention. She turned to face the stranger.

'Please,' he said. 'There is no time.'

Swayed by his insistence the old woman followed the man down a byroad that she had never paid much attention to or travelled on before. They passed nobody on the road. In fact there was a silence in the air that she had never experienced before. There wasn't even the sound of bird song. The road narrowed so that not even a cart could squeeze through but there before her rose up a small cottage with a wisp of smoke rising into the air.

The man opened the door but the widow could see very little in the dim light of the cottage. When the door closed behind them her eyes began to adjust and she saw the young woman lying on a low bed near the fire. She walked towards her but stopped suddenly. She was about to cry out when the young woman put her finger to her lips and gave her a warning glare.

'Daughter,' she whispered to herself. She had to put her hand out to the fireplace to steady herself.

It was her daughter who was supposed be dead. What was she doing here? And why was she shooting her glares of warning? The widow walked nervously towards the bed. She wanted to throw her arms around her daughter but all she could do was grasp her hand.

As the man busied himself at the fire the widow's daughter pulled her mother close to explain.

'He's a fairy man and we're married mother,' she said. 'It was the fairies who took me away and left a changeling in my place.'

'Oh darling,' the woman said.

'You mustn't let on that you know who I am. Just help me as if I'm a stranger,' the daughter said. 'When the baby comes he will want to give you a reward for your help. You must refuse but ask instead to take the boy home with you. He'll refuse but if you beg earnestly, he will give him to you in the end.'

The mother attended her daughter and thankfully everything went without a hitch. Once the baby had been washed, swaddled in a warm blanket and in his mother's arms, the widow set about tidying up.

'I must thank you for your kindness and for tending to my wife,' the fairy man said. 'It is only right that I reward you with anything that you wish for.'

The widow did her best to act naturally. 'Oh there is nothing in this world that I need but I implore you to give that beautiful boy into my care and I will raise him to be a fine strong man.'

'I'm not going to give up my own son,' he said.

'He'd be better off with me and you know that,' she said.

Of course it is often the case that the fairies leave their own children to be reared by ordinary folk. The man looked at his wife but she seemed totally distracted.

'Please,' the woman said. 'I can give him everything that he needs.'

The fairy man relented and said she could take the boy with her. 'But mark my words, if I get wind that he's not being treated right you'll regret the very day you met me,' he said.

The widow walked over to the bed to lift the boy out of his mother's arms. Her daughter's face was mingled with sadness and joy. As the widow lifted the child the daughter slipped a magic ring into her hand and whispered, 'When it glows you'll know we are about and we can meet on the hill behind the house,' she said. 'But if you ever see my husband you must never acknowledge him or me.'

The old woman returned home with the red-haired boy, her grandson. 'Oh, that is a lovely healthy boy,' her neighbour said the next day.

'He's the son of a niece of mine who lives down in Sligo. She's poorly after the birth and I offered to take care of him,' she said.

'Well he couldn't be in better hands,' the neighbour said. And the child became accepted in the community.

The widow kept the ring safely and whenever it glowed she would take the child up onto the hill behind the house and spent time with her daughter. They treasured their time together and it brought them such joy. The widow had to be careful when she was in the town because there were times when she could see her daughter with her fairy husband.

All the years of sadness were slowly lifting off the old woman's shoulders and she walked taller than she had in years.

Then one day, with her heart full of joy, she met her daughter and her husband at the fair day in Glenties. The red-haired boy was clinging to her arms and without thinking she said a big hello to them.

'How can you see me?' the fairy man asked. There was fury burning in his eyes and before she could think of an explanation the man blew on her eyes and she could no longer see the fairies. The precious ring also disappeared and she never saw her daughter again.

The common version of this story involves the woman rubbing an ointment onto the baby and inadvertently rubbing her eye. She meets the fairy folk at the market and sees them out of one eye. When the fairy man asks if she can see them with both eyes she said no, just the right one. The fairy man then pokes her eye out and she is blind in that eye for the rest of her days.

FEAR DARRIG
IN DONEGAL

Pat Diver, a tinker man, was well accustomed to a wandering life, and to strange shelters; he had shared the beggar's blanket in smoky cabins; he had crouched beside the still in many a nook and corner where poteen was made on the wild Inishowen mountains; he had even slept on the bare heather, or in the ditch, with no roof over him but the vault of heaven; yet all his nights of adventure were tame and commonplace when compared with the night I'm going to tell you about.

Pat had spent the day mending all the kettles and saucepans in Moville and Greencastle and was on the road to Culdaff when he was overtaken by the night on a lonely mountain road. As was the custom of the day he knocked at one door after another.

'Is there a chance of resting beneath your roof on this night?' he asked, jingling the halfpenny in his pocket.

But to his surprise at each house he received the same answer, a very definite 'no'.

'Where's the boasted hospitality of Inishowen?' he asked at one door but his only answer was a loud thud as the door shut.

'What's the use of being able to pay for your board when the people seem so churlish?' he thought to himself.

He stood wondering what he was going to do for the night when he spotted a light twinkling off the main track. He made his way towards the small cottage, hoping against hope that he would get shelter. He spied through the window an old man and woman sitting on each side of the fire.

He knocked gently on the door.

'Will you be pleased to give me a night's lodging, sir?' Pat asked respectfully.

'Can you tell a story?' asked the old man.

'I'm afraid I'm no great storyteller,' replied Pat, even more puzzled.

'Then you may go on a bit further for only one that can tell a story will get in here,' the old man said.

The tone of the old man's reply was so definite that Pat did not attempt to repeat his request but turned away to resume his weary journey.

'A story, indeed,' he muttered to the night sky. 'Old wives' tales to please the weans.'

As he bent to pick up his bundle of tinkering implements he spotted a barn standing a way off behind the house. He made his way across to it. He opened the barn door and with the light of the moon he could see a clean, roomy barn with a heap of straw in the corner. It was a lot better than the shelter he had had on many a night and he crept happily under the straw. He was asleep in minutes.

Pat was awoken within a short time by the heavy tramp of feet. Peeping cautiously through a gap in the pile of straw he saw four immensely tall men entering the barn. Pat's eyes widened as he saw them dragging a body behind them which they threw roughly into the middle of the barn. They made such a racket that he expected the old man to appear at any minute but the barn door banged shut and stayed so.

The next thing he knew, the men were lighting a fire in the middle of the barn. They fastened the corpse by the feet with a great rope to a beam in the roof dangling in front of the fire. One of the men started turning the body before the fire.

After a time the man was sheathed in a sweat from his labours and he called to a gigantic fellow, the tallest of the four:

'Come on, I'm tired. It's time for you to take your turn,' he said.

'And why would I turn him,' replied the big man, 'when there's Pat Diver under the straw and he could take my turn.'

With hideous clamour the four men called poor Pat who was terrified beyond terror. Seeing there was no escape Pat thought it was wisest to come forth as he was bidden.

'Now Pat,' they said, 'you'll turn the corpse but if you let him burn you'll be tied up there yourself and roasted in his place.'

Pat's hair stood on end and cold sweat poured from his forehead and his clothes were soon clinging fast to his skin. There was nothing for it but to perform the dreadful task.

Seeing Pat stuck into his task the four men departed, leaving him to continue alone. But soon the flames rose higher and higher so that it burnt the rope, bringing the corpse down with a crash, scattering ashes and embers across the barn floor. The miserable cook let out a howl of anguish as he took to his feet and ran for his life.

Pat ran on along the road until he was close to collapse when he spied a drain overgrowing with tall, rank grass. He thought that it was the perfect place to creep into and lie hidden till morning.

He lay there stock-still with terror, trying to erase the scenes he had just witnessed. No matter how hard he tried his nostrils kept filling with the smell of burning flesh. He thought he would lose his mind, if not indeed his life, lying in that drain.

But it was only minutes that he was lying in the drain being tortured before he heard the heavy tramping of feet. He spied his four tormentors coming towards him, one of them carrying their burden. The man stopped and laid the corpse on the edge of the drain.

'I'm tired,' said the one carrying the corpse to the giant, 'it's your turn to carry him a piece.'

'And why would I carry him,' he said 'when there's Pat Diver in the drain and he can take my turn?'

'Come out Pat, come out Pat,' roared all the men as one.

Almost dead with fright Pat crept out to face his nightmare.

'Now Pat,' they said, 'carry that corpse to its grave and if you let him fall it will be you in his place.'

He staggered under the weight of the corpse, doing his best not to collapse. His legs were close to giving way when he saw his four tall companions turning towards Kiltown Abbey. The abbey was a ruin festooned with ivy where the only sound was the owl hooting and the screech of the bat. The long-forgotten dead slept peacefully around the walls under the dense tangle of brambles. Pat knew that no one was ever buried there now but the four started digging in the wild graveyard.

Pat, seeing them thus engaged, thought he might once more to try to escape. He looked about for any way to get away and, spotting a hawthorn in the fence, he climbed up into the boughs hoping to be hidden from his tormentors. From his hiding place he watched the men take turns at digging the grave.

'I'm tired,' said the man who was digging, 'here, take the spade,' addressing the big man; 'it's your turn.'

'And why would I be digging,' he asked 'when there's Pat Diver in the boughs and he can take my turn?'

Pat came down to take the spade but just then the cocks in the little farmyards and cottages round the abbey began to crow. The men looked at one another.

'We must go now Pat,' they said, 'and well it is for you that the cocks crowed for if they had not, you'd be going into that grave with the corpse.'

The four men disappeared before his eyes. Pat looked about trying to see what direction the four had headed. There was no trace of them anywhere. Without delay he took to his heels and headed away from the scene of his nightmare.

Pat went on about his travels mending pots and kettles around Carndonagh, Buncrana and beyond. Pat wasn't sure whether to believe what he had witnessed himself. He had no evidence to show except the terror that still coursed through his veins. He decided to say nothing of the night on his travels.

Two months had passed and Pat was beginning to feel more like himself. He had travelled wide and far across Donegal when he found himself in Raphoe on a fair day.

Pat stopped suddenly when he saw the big man among the crowd that filled the Diamond.

'How are you now Pat Diver?' asked the big man, bending down to look into the tinker's face.

'You've the advantage of me, sir, for I haven't had the pleasure of meeting you,' faltered Pat.

'Do you not know me Pat?' he asked. The big man bent down to whisper in Pat's ear. 'When you go back to Inishowen you'll have a story to tell now.'

12

CHANGELING

In years gone by people did many things to protect their children from the fairy folk. It was known that the fairies travelled about seeking to snatch a child, leaving a changeling in its place. People did many things to protect their children from such interference. Boys were often clothed in dresses to hide their identity. For a girl, the mother or grandmother would place an iron poker from the fireside over the cot, or some other piece of iron, for that metal is always obnoxious to the fairies.

There was a man who lived near Croghan Fort, not far from Lifford, who was short and had a cataract – or as the country people call it, a pearl – on his eye. Now that part of the country had a long and ancient history and was known to have been the birthplace of several High Kings of Ireland.

One night he was returning home not long after the birth of his child. Well, he couldn't believe his eyes when he met a troop of fairies coming up the road carrying off his own infant. They were about to change a bentwood into the likeness of the child while chanting:

'Make it wee, make it short;
Make it like its own folk;

Put a pearl in its eye;
Make it like its Daddy.'

The man interrupted them by throwing up sand and exclaiming: 'In the name of God, this to you and mine to me.'

The fairies turned and threw the baby at him but it fell to the ground and broke its hip or thigh, and from that day was a cripple all its life.

13

FAIRY WANDERING

Paddy McHugh lived just outside Ramelton near Tully Mountain. He spent his day working the small bit of land he owned. But at night his life was transformed for he was known wide and far for his melodeon playing. His rough working hands were transformed and his nimble fingers on the keys would set any crowd to dancing. As a result he was in great demand for dances, parties, weddings and even wakes. Many were the nights he found himself walking home with only the moon and stars for company.

One day he met his neighbour standing looking at an old tree that stood to the side of the house. 'I'm going to take this tree down Paddy,' he said. 'It's ugly and blocks the light on this side of the house.'

'Well I wouldn't touch that tree,' said Paddy. 'That tree is a fairy tree and if you interfere with it they will cause you nothing but trouble.'

Now Paddy was used to listening to stories as he went about playing his music and many's the musician that related a story of hearing a tune after an encounter with the wee folk.

'Ah, don't give me that,' his neighbour said. 'It's only an auld excuse for a tree and I'm tired looking at it.'

'Well you've be warned,' Paddy said.

One night, after a great dance in Ramelton, Paddy was making his way home towards Tully Mountain. He felt he had been walking for hours and a great tiredness was settling on his shoulders.

He stopped to look about, feeling that his home was close by but despite looking in every direction he couldn't make out any familiar landmark. He wandered about in search of some hint that he was near home.

Eventually he grew so tired that he decided to rest his legs and found a comfortable place to sit with his back resting against a tree. Well it wasn't long before his heavy lids shut themselves and he was fast asleep.

Suddenly his eyes flashed open as he felt a sharp pain across his rear end. He was running wildly around the field and he had a weight on his back that wasn't his melodeon. He raced around in circles feeling a sharp whack on his back.

'Whips and spurs for Paddy McHugh,' he heard the cry go up. How long he raced around the field he had no idea but as soon as one of the wee folk had had his fun another jumped on his back, he felt the whack of the whip and the call went up; 'Whips and spurs for Paddy McHugh.'

Paddy woke with a start. His body ached all over. He had fallen asleep on his feet and he didn't know when the whip had stopped its onslaught and the wee folk had got off his back. His melodeon was cast aside on the ground. He looked around himself and realised that his own home was just over the hedge from where he had been tortured. He lifted his melodeon and gingerly picked his way home.

Later the next day he met his neighbour. Paddy's back ached and his rear end stung. Despite his discomfort he saw the dark cloud on his neighbour's face.

'You look like you've had bad news,' said Paddy.

'You won't believe it but I found all my pigs dead today,' the neighbour said.

'How could that have happened?' asked Paddy. 'Were they attacked?'

'No. I just found them dead.'

Paddy didn't know what to say. And then it struck him.

'Did you by any chance cut that tree?' said Paddy.

'I did, but you're not going to tell me that's the cause of my pigs dying,' said his neighbour.

'Well I had the strangest night ever and it could only have been the wee folk. They were abroad last night and they weren't very friendly,' said Paddy.

He then told his neighbour of the strange events of the night before. His neighbour shook his head as he listened. Could this be true? He knew his neighbour well and knew him to be a reliable man. He wasn't one for wild speculating and even though he was fond of dances he knew he wasn't one for drink.

'Maybe I should have listened to you Paddy,' said the neighbour.

14

JAMIE FRIEL

On the Fanad peninsula there stands the ruin of a castle that is said to come to life every Halloween night. Now that can only mean one thing – the fairies, the wee folk. Halloween is one of the nights when they move freely in the world. People do what is best and avoid the place. Most people will know that messing with the wee folk usually brings nothing but trouble.

Now on one Halloween night, a young man who lived near the ruined castle sat looking at the flames in the peat fire. There was no sound in his small cottage but the young man was growing restless. He couldn't help his mind wandering to the she-nanigans that were going on up at the castle. Now don't think for one minute that this young man was foolish – far from it. He was wise beyond his years. Maybe it was because he had become the head of the household at a young age when his father passed away. More likely it was his keen wit, sharp mind and the glint in his eye.

The dog yelped when he rose suddenly.

'What's ailing you Jamie Friel this evening?' asked his mother.

'I thought I'd take a bit of walk to stretch the legs,' he said.

'Well don't go messing around that castle, you hear me. I know that head of yours and it's just the sort of foolish thing you would do.'

'Ah mother I'm no fool; I thought you knew that by now,' he said.

'Aye, that's true but sometimes you can do awful foolish things Jamie Friel,' she said. 'You'll only bring a lock of trouble on yours and my head messing with that crowd.'

'Don't be worrying that old head of yours then. I'll be back before you know it.'

Of course the castle was the very place he was headed. Since he first heard the stories of the castle he had wanted to see what it was that the wee folk got up to. Why this year? Who can answer that? Why does the branch break when one more snow-drop falls?

As Jamie approached the castle he could hear the music, the sound of dancing and voices raised in revelry. He stopped to listen for a moment. The music was as magic as he had heard. He wondered if he should step inside but once the music had wrapped itself around him he no longer had a choice.

'Jamie Friel, Jamie Friel,
welcome from me and welcome to thee.
Be friend to me and I'll be a friend to thee,
Be a foe to me and I'll bring you nothing but woe.'

Jamie looked about stunned that anyone knew his name or that he was approaching. He stepped into the glow of the lamplight to see a small but powerful man standing in front of him in greeting.

'We've been expecting you for some time Jamie Friel and we are glad you came. Enjoy the music, the dancing and the food.'

Jamie soon found himself in the middle of all that was hap-pening. He was dancing even though he wasn't one to dance. He sang a song which had never passed his lips before and he tasted the most wonderful food ever. Jamie had no sense of time passing but he was pulled from his reverie when the music suddenly stopped and the fairies gathered in a large circle in the middle of the clearing. In the distance he heard the church bell ring out midnight. He shook his head in disbelief but before his thoughts could settle his attention was drawn to the sky.

Descending from the air were twenty small winged horses that landed gently before him. A fairy jumped onto the back of each white horse.

> Jamie Friel Jamie Friel
> Will you not come with me?
> Sights to behold
> And wonders to see.

Now Jamie had heard all the stories about the wee folk and he knew in his heart of hearts that this would end badly. But curiosity is a wonderful gift and a terrible curse. Which it is we often can't tell until it's over, whenever that might be.

Jamie jumped up on to a spare winged horse and they took to the air.

Such sights greeted his eyes from the air. He had never seen the land before from such an elevated position, as unnatural images and flight were unknown in his time.

He blinked away the tears that the cold air produced in his eyes. Below him an arrangement of small lights dotted the landscape as if attempting to mirror the night sky. A full moon hung in the sky allowing him to see the undulations of the countryside below. Some of the features he could make out. In a short time the smell of the salt air filled his nostrils as they flew over Lough Swilly. On and on the horses galloped through the air.

'Where are we going?' he asked.

All he heard in reply was a devilish laugh.

Mountains rose up before them and the horses rose higher in the air to surmount them. Not long after the land stretched out like a giant patchwork quilt, interrupted by rivers, lakes and forests. He felt he could see the whole country laid out before him.

On and on they flew. Now Jamie had never travelled further than the 20 miles to the fair in Letterkenny. How far he had now travelled he had no idea. Lights blinked upwards to him and at times larger clusters appeared marking a town. He couldn't tell how long they had been in the air but in the distance he could see what looked like a fireball ahead and the horses were heading straight for it.

'Stop! Please stop,' he shouted to the fairies. 'We'll die in the fire. Please. I have my mother to take care of.'

Howls of laughter erupted about him and onwards galloped the horses.

Soon they were upon the fiery mass and Jamie's panic eased as the shapes of houses revealed themselves and the flames tamed to street lamps.

'Is this Dublin?' he asked.

'Indeed it is,' he said. 'A place of great excitement and high jinks.'

Now Jamie didn't give too much thought to what the fairies had planned. His eyes darted about taking in the sights of the great city as it lay sleeping below, bathed in a ghostly light. He had heard all sorts of stories about city life and hoped he would be safe from the demons that lurked below.

Suddenly the horses began to descend. He could see a large square below him, a green area in the middle surrounded by large imposing houses. It was St Stephen's Green in the heart of Dublin, known to all who have visited the city as a place of quiet refuge from the hustle and bustle. In those days it was also home to many rich families who lived in the houses that surround it.

The horses landed silently and the fairies jumped lightly from their mounts.

'Come Jamie Friel and see what mischief we have in mind for you tonight,' said the leader of the fairies.

It was only now that Jamie felt any alarm. He hadn't thought that he was to be involved in any mischief.

They had landed right outside one of the fine houses. Some of the fairies jumped onto the windowsill while Jamie strained his neck to see through. Inside, the room was immersed in soft lamplight. Jamie could see three people huddled in a tight group with their heads hanging.

One of the men shook his head and he heard the distressed cries of the woman. The other man gripped her as she fainted and they quickly carried her from the room. It was only then that Jamie saw the beautiful young woman lying in the bed. Her face was so pale that it looked as if the moon had climbed down to shine out of her. He was entranced by her beauty. But then he saw her lips. Not the bright red lips of healthy young woman but blue-tinged lips that showed the lurking of death.

Before he had time to say anything the fairies had lifted the window. Jamie watched as they went into the room, pulled back the blankets and lifted her limp body from the bed. They carried her to the window.

'Take her Jamie Friel,' the fairy told him.

Jamie hesitated for a moment unsure of what he was doing.

'Hurry up,' the fairy urged him and Jamie responded to the command.

Jamie took the young woman in his arms and gazed at her beautiful face.

'She a beauty alright,' said the fairy, 'but hurry we don't have time for admiring now.'

Jamie glanced through the window and was amazed to see the young woman lying back in her bed. 'But how could that be?' he wondered feeling her weight in his arms. The he realised it was a changeling left in her stead.

'Are you going to stand gawping all night or are you coming home with us,' called the fairy.

Jamie ran and mounted his horse, holding tightly to the young woman. The horses rose into the air and began their long journey back to Fanad. Jamie noticed little of the changing world below. Instead he watched the young woman as she lay sleeping in his arms. He marvelled at her beauty and wondered about her parents. What was it they would find in the bed when they returned to the room?

Onwards the steeds beat their wings towards home and before he knew it he could see the waters of Lough Swilly below him.

'I have to do something,' he thought to himself.

'It has been a fine night of fun and mischief,' said the leader of the fairies, 'and we have you to thank above all Jamie Friel. I hope you have enjoyed yourself and we'll be forever in your pay.'

Jamie thought of the beautiful young girl in his arms. What would become of her? A life with the fairies below ground? No sunshine or other human to speak with? And what about her poor parents in Dublin left with a changeling? Jamie knew he had to do something. He couldn't allow this.

As the horses landed hard on the ground in front of the castle ruins Jamie leapt from the horse holding the young woman tight in his arms. He took to his heels, racing towards home and away from the stunned fairies.

'Jamie Friel, Jamie Friel, we made you welcome and now you betray us.'

Before he was out of sight an old woman among the fairies began muttering a curse on Jamie for his betrayal. Jamie ran as fast as he could away from the spot, towards home. When he arrived at his home the lights were all out while a few embers burned in the grate. Jamie placed the young woman gently in a chair. He ran to light the lamp and stoke the fire.

'Good God where have you been Jamie Friel and what sort of trouble have you brought on this house,' Jamie's mother cried from the door.

'Oh mother I had to do something. The fairies took this young woman from her home in Dublin and were going to keep her under the ground with them.'

'Dublin! I warned you not to go near that crowd this night,' she said.

'I know, I know, but I had to help her,' said Jamie.

'She's as white as a ghost,' said his mother.

'She was sick in bed when they took her. I think she might be dying,' said Jamie.

'What? And what are we supposed to do? Indeed what am I supposed to tell the neighbours? And the priest!'

They put her in the spare room at the back of the house and lit the fire there. Over the coming weeks the mother helped nurse the young woman back to health. And when she was fully fit Jamie and his mother discovered that the young woman was deaf and dumb. But she had not always been so. Jamie discovered that it was only since the night the fairies took her. Had the fairies done something or was it because of her illness? Jamie had not heard the words of the old woman but it was indeed her words that had brought silence to the young woman.

In some ways this was a blessing for Jamie's mother as it made it easier to explain the presence of the young woman, saying she was a distant relative that needed shelter.

Once back to health the young woman became part of the household, helping with the chores and enjoying the company of Jamie and his mother. She was frustrated by her inability to communicate freely but they found their own ways. Of course she missed her home but Jamie didn't have the means to return her to her family. They all settled into an easy routine around each other and life was good to them. It wasn't long before a year had passed and it was Halloween again. Jamie was on edge the whole day, a fact that didn't go unnoticed by his mother.

'Jamie Friel, I hope you not planning on going near those fairies again. You brought enough trouble on us last year,' his mother said.

'It won't be any trouble,' he said as he headed out the door.

He could hear her pleading as he walked away from the cottage, unsure of what he was doing or expecting to happen. He walked slowly to the castle where he had met the fairies the previous year. Soon he heard the sound of music and merriment. He crept slowly towards the entrance and listened carefully.

Above the din he heard a croaky voice say 'Ha! That Jamie Friel tricking us last year. But I settled him. I put a spell on her that means she's deaf and dumb.'

There was a great guffaw of laughter.

'And if he only knew that with a sip of this, she would be fine again.'

There was another burst of laughter and Jamie moved to see what the old woman was talking about. He could see her holding up a golden cup that she passed on to her neighbour. He knew what he had to do. He stepped into the glow of the lamplight and silence fell on the gathering.

> Well Jamie Friel, Jamie Friel,
>
> We made you welcome,
>
> But you turned on your heel.
>
> I hope you haven't come here to try to trick us again?

'I'm sorry for that,' said Jamie, 'but sure that one was no good to you anyway, she can't speak or hear a thing!' There was a great burst of laughter.

'Well you didn't think we would let you off with a thing like that did you?' said the fairy.

'I wondered about that,' he said. 'But as I say, I only came to say sorry and to drink your health.'

'I guess you've suffered enough,' said the fairy.

'And will suffer for a long time to come,' said the old woman with a wicked grin on her face.' There was more laughter from the assembled fairies.

The music started up again and Jamie was soon in the middle of the crowd dancing like he never danced before. But as he moved with the music he kept a sharp eye on the golden cup that the fairies passed from one to the other. When the chance came he grabbed the cup but instead of drinking from it he ran as fast as his legs would take him from the castle towards home, covering the cup so as not to spill the precious liquid. He was well out of sight before the fairies realised what had happened but he could hear their shouts fade into the background.

'What trouble have you brought with you this time Jamie Friel?' his mother said as he burst through the door.

'Oh, no trouble mother but the answer to one of our problems.'

He gave the goblet to the young woman and explained all to his mother as she drank.

Well, there was great celebration when the young woman finished her drink. She could speak and hear clearly. Jamie explained everything that had happened with the fairies. After being trapped inside her own head for so long the young woman, whose name was Annie, couldn't stop talking till the night turned to day. She told them everything about herself and her family. She told them how thankful she was to them for taking care of her. And of course how she longed to return home and to see her dear parents.

Jamie didn't know what to say to this request. While they had food enough to live on they had little money to undertake such a journey. After a number of days it was clear to Jamie that he had to find a way to take Annie back to her parents. He gathered together what little money he had and said they could set out but would have to walk most of the way.

They made the long journey to Dublin, which took over a week. When they arrived at St Stephen's Green people stared at them; their simple clothes contrasted greatly with the rich fabrics of the square, especially after a hard week of travelling. When they arrived at Annie's house Jamie wanted to leave her but she insisted he stay to meet her parents.

'Yes?' asked the butler as he held the door half open, looking down his nose on the two at the door.

'It's me, Annie,' Annie said.

'Annie who?' asked the Butler.

'Oh Michael, it's me, Annie, don't you recognise me?' she asked.

'How dare you Miss, come here pretending to be Annie. If you don't clear away I'll call the police,' the Butler said.

'Please Michael,' she pleaded. 'Tell Mother and Father I'm here.'

The door suddenly opened. Standing in the doorway was Annie's father who had been attracted to the door by the raised voices.

'Oh Father, it's me, Annie,' she said, as she stepped to embrace him.

'What is the meaning of this?' he cried in anger and pushed her away. 'My Annie died a year ago. How could you come here to cause upset?'

Annie and Jamie tried to explain what had happened with the fairies but as you can imagine it was a fantastical story.

'Please Father, call mother, she will recognise me,' Annie demanded.

Just then her mother appeared at the door. She gasped in horror when she saw the two ragged figures at the door.

'Oh mother,' said Annie, 'it's me, Annie. They won't believe me but I know you will.'

'How can this be? My baby is dead,' she said.

Then Annie pulled back her coat and pulled the top of her dress down over her left shoulder, revealing a distinctive birthmark that was shaped like a heart.

'How can it be?' her mother said, as she felt faint and held on to her husband.

Annie and Jamie were taken inside and told the whole story to the shocked parents. They found it hard to believe what they heard, but the evidence was there before them as their Annie was alive and well, not cold in the grave they had attended for over a year.

Annie's parents didn't know how they were going to thank Jamie for all he had done but Annie knew exactly how she wanted to thank him. When Jamie announced that he should be getting back to his home, Annie asked him to marry her. And indeed they did get married and lived a long and happy life together. And Jamie was sure to never cross paths with the fairy folk again.

15

THE OUTSMARTING
OF CONAL DOHERTY

Conal Doherty lived for one thing and that was to have fun. He avoided work whenever he could and put all his efforts into going to parties and dances, whether on a fair day or some occasion that a family was celebrating. He always dressed in his best attire for such occasions; his Donegal tweed three-piece suit with a dapper handkerchief peeping non-chalantly from its breast pocket. Some said he was a dashing-looking character but others who were of a less generous disposition, and it has to be said there were many of those about, said he had notions above his station. Seemingly a desire to better oneself was greatly frowned upon!

Conal was lucky because his father had been a hard-working man and had built up a sizeable amount of land and had resources enough to pay men to work. Now Conal had inherited the land and was determined to live on its fruit. However, unlike his father, he wasn't prepared to work hard so in time the place started to look shabby, and then some of the fields were left go fallow for lack of labour. In time he couldn't afford to employ as many men and things went further downhill. Even his tweed suit started to show a bit of wear and tear. But Conal was content enough as long as he could go and enjoy himself at a dance or party.

One winter's evening he was heading in to Ramelton for a dance. It was a beautiful crisp cold night with a half moon hanging in the sky to light his way with ease. He was well wrapped up against the cold and whistling to himself, thinking of the sport that lay ahead.

Suddenly he heard a tapping noise coming from the hedge. It interrupted his tune with its insistence and he stopped to listen.

'What could that be?' he thought to himself. It wasn't a bird and he couldn't imagine any wee creature out on cold night like this.

His curiosity aroused, he crept over to the hedge to take a closer look. Well, he couldn't believe his eyes when he spied a wee leprechaun busy within, making a pair of shoes.

'Well this is my lucky night,' he thought. 'If I catch him I'll get his gold and I'll be a rich man.'

As he was thinking this he remembered the stories his own father had told him as a child about the leprechaun. They always had to tell you the truth, and there was something else. But what was it? He couldn't recall but sure the main thing was the wee fellow would have to answer his question and he would have his gold.

He rolled back his sleeve and shot his hand in like a bullet.

'Let me go, let me go,' cried the wee man, trying desperately to free himself.

'Whist you now and answer my question true and you and I can be on our way,' said Conal.

'And what would that be then?' asked the Leprechaun.

'I think you know full well what that question is,' said Conal.

'Oh now, I wouldn't a go second-guessing a clever and dapper man like you.'

Now Conal didn't know whether he was trying to flatter him or make fun of him.

'Come now and tell me where your gold is?' said Conal.

'Gold,' said the wee man. 'Is that all you people ever think about? You'd never ask me for a fine pair of shoes to go with that suit of yours. Fine shoes to set you dancing.'

'When I get my hands on your gold I can buy the finest shoes in the land,' retorted Conal.

'Ha! All the gold you can find couldn't buy the shoes I could make you.'

'Why, they must be a fine pair of shoes indeed and I have no doubt that one with your skill could create such a thing, but really it's gold I'm after.'

Now it was the wee man's turn to wonder if Conal was trying to flatter him or make fun of him.

'I don't have any gold!' said the Leprechaun

'Now friend, don't take me for a fool,' said Conal. 'You know you have to tell me the truth so tell me where it is.'

'Right so,' said he. 'It's over yonder behind that hedge on the far side.'

Conal was just about to look when it came to him what was that other piece of advice his father had given to him about the wee folk; 'keep looking in their eyes for if you glance away for even the quickest time the wee man will disappear and take his gold with him.'

'I'm not falling for that one boyo,' said Conal. 'You'll show the way and I'll keep my eye on yours.'

The wee man led Conal across the road and into the field over yonder. Once inside he pointed to a spot on the ground, 'There's your gold, buried under that stalk of ragweed.'

'And how am I supposed to get it up from there?' demanded Conal.

'Sure you can get one of your men to do it if you're not up to it yourself,' said the wee man. 'Or maybe you can't afford to have him out at this time.'

'Now boy you're not going to get a rise out of me,' said Conal. 'Do you not have a shovel that I can use?'

'I'm a shoemaker not a gardener,' said the wee man.

'Ah and so you are,' said Conal trying to placate him. 'I'll have to go up to the farm and get a shovel. But hold on now, does that mean you can move my gold on me?'

'No no. It will stay in that spot until the sun climbs into the sky in the morning.'

'Well thank you then kind sir,' said Conal as he let the man go.

'You can keep your thanks for sure, taking a wee man's fortune like that and you not willing to do a bit of work.'

Conal stood looking at the spot rubbing his hands with joy. He'd probably miss the dance but there would be plenty of dancing and parties once he had his gold. In fact the first thing he would do is have a huge Christmas party in his own house that would be the envy of the whole area, of the rich and the poor. But just as he was about to move off didn't he notice that there wasn't just one ragweed in the field. In fact, the whole field was covered in them.

'Damn and blast,' he roared into the air. 'How am I to know which one it is now?'

Then he remembered the handkerchief in his pocket. He whipped it out and tied it onto the weed. It was his favourite blue one made of silk but he didn't mind as he could buy as many as he wanted with his new-found wealth.

He skipped up the road to get a shovel. He had to search for a while as he hadn't used one in some time. Once located, he couldn't get back to the field quick enough and gave no thought to changing out of his fine clothes. He jumped into the field, saw the weed with his handkerchief on and started digging.

For a man who hadn't used a shovel in a long time he made a great dent in the earth in a short time but soon he slowed as he struggled to dig deeper to find his gold. He dug and dug long into the night like a body possessed. How long he was digging he had no idea or care but he seemed no closer to finding his gold. He stopped to wipe his brow and to take stock. He glanced up and couldn't believe it.

'Well damn and double blast,' he cursed, for the sun was up. 'How can this be?' he shouted to the clouds above.

He threw the shovel out of the hole and climbed up himself. It was a long enough climb as he had made a right deep crater in the field. When at last he was free of the hole he looked about him.

'Well, curses on that wee fellow anyway,' said Conal, as he spied a blue silk handkerchief on every weed in the field.

'And curses on me too,' he said as he realised it was his own field that he had long neglected.

Not to be totally outdone he went around the field and gathered up the silk handkerchiefs. As he un-knotted each one he wondered to himself if it was the one that had the gold beneath. Of course there was no point digging now as the wee man would have moved the gold as the first rays of day brushed the sky. When he had done the round of the field he picked up his shovel and headed up the road home to get some sleep. As he passed out through the gate he thought he heard tittering in the ditch beside him.

'You might have tricked me this time wee man but if I get my hands on you again I'll get my gold,' Conal shouted to the air. But as he looked at the sorry field covered in weeds he recalled another piece of advice his father had given him:

'If you work hard and take care of the farm, it will give you all you need.'

He realised that it wasn't the leprechaun who had done him out of his gold but his own laziness. He vowed to work on the farm and if by chance he encountered the wee man again his fields wouldn't be full of weeds for him to outsmart him.

16

THE DROWNING WAVE

Seanie Doherty kept a boat on the lake near his home and would spend many hours on it fishing. It was a great place to contemplate his life and to find some peace and quiet away from his busy life. One fine day, with the sun high in the sky and the land lying still, he headed down to the lake to go fishing. As he walked he met his neighbour Donal who often accompanied him on the lake.

'Are you coming with me today Donal, for the season will be over soon?' said Seanie.

'Surely,' said he, 'and it's a grand day to be out too.'

They pushed the boat into the water, jumped in and grabbed hold of the oars. They rowed out to the middle of the lake and cast their lines. It was one of those days when there wasn't a whisper of wind nor a ripple of water. Each and every sound from the land drifted across the water and they felt they were part of the activities and conversations of the day. They sat in the boat facing each other, feeling their lines for any bites, but lost in their own thoughts.

Suddenly Seanie jumped to his feet, his face ashen white and pointing over the shoulder of Donal. His mouth was gaping and flapping like a fish lying in the bottom of the boat. Donal didn't need him to tell him what was happening as he could hear it. Although he couldn't believe it, he could hear a wave crashing towards the boat. He glanced over his shoulder to see the huge wave closing in, ready to swallow them up.

Seanie stood stock still but somewhere in his mind the thread of a story wove its way to consciousness. He bent down and picked up the knife that they had in the bottom of the boat for fishing. It had a long silver blade and a blue handle. Seanie gripped the knife between his fingers and let it fly at the wave with all his strength. As the knife plunged into the wave it dropped and died before their eyes.

'What just happened? Donal asked. 'Why did you throw the knife? Why did it stop?'

'I've no idea,' said Seanie. 'I didn't realise I was even doing it but I'm mighty glad I did.'

With that they took in their lines, heaved to at the oars and headed back to shore.

'What do we tell our wives?' wondered Donal.

'What can we tell?' said Seanie. 'They'll think we're crazy if we tell them what happened, or at least won't believe us.'

'You're right there,' said Donal.

They headed back to their own homes and all that evening each of their wives asked what was wrong.

'Did you have a falling out?'

'What happened today, for you're fierce strange this evening?'

But Seanie and Donal just dismissed the questions and went to their beds early that night. It was little sleep they could get and because of it Seanie heard a light tapping on his door at midnight. He climbed out of bed trying not to wake the house and went down to see who it was. He was expecting to see Donal in much the same state as himself. When he opened the door he could see no one. But his attention was drawn to the ground when he heard a voice speak up to him: 'You must come with me for my daughter is dying.'

He looked down to see a small old man standing pleadingly. 'It's a doctor you need then,' said Seanie.

'It's not a doctor that can save her but only your hand. Please,' he said.

Well, whether it was because he couldn't sleep or because of the strange day he had had, Seanie took his coat off the hook and followed the wee man. He led him out beyond the village and towards the hills. It was a clear night with a fine moon and Seanie had clear sight of the countryside around him. It all looked familiar yet as he walked he felt he had no idea where he was.

By and by he saw a small cottage in front of him with a line of white smoke drifting into the sky. He had to bend low to get in through the door and when he stepped inside he was nearly driven back by the roaring fire that was in it despite the warm night. There on a low bed beside the fire he saw a beautiful young woman with skin as white as the winter snows. Her lips too were a deathly white. The wee man walked over to the bed and lifted the blanket.

Poor Seanie nearly fainted when he saw the wound in her leg with a blue-handled knife with a long silver blade sticking out of it. The very knife he had thrown at the wave that day. And then he remembered a story he had once heard of the 'Drowning Wave' and how such a wave was a fairy trying to take some poor unfortunate over to their side.

Well, without hesitation Seanie gripped the blue handle and pulled the knife from her leg. As he watched, the wound healed over and he saw colour rush to her cheeks and her lips redden.

'Thank you,' said the wee man. 'You have saved her life.'

'But she nearly took ours today,' said Seanie.

'Ah but we don't end life, just bring you to a different one,' said the fairy man.

'Much the same really,' said Seanie.

'Well have no worry. Due to your kindness the wave won't appear again in these parts.'

With that the wee man led Seanie back home. The next day he went to visit Donal and told him about the strange events of the night before. When he finished the tale they decided it was best to keep it to themselves. But sure enough, somewhere along the ling one of them said it to someone and that someone told someone else until someone else eventually told me and now I'm telling you.

And true to their word the fairies didn't visit the lake again and the Drowning Wave hasn't been seen since.

17

PADDY THE PIPER

It was the summer of the 'ruction when the long summer days, like the days of many a fine fellow's precious life, were cut short by reason of the martial law. When the day's work was over, a decent lad couldn't be out of an evening, whether it be good or bad he was up to. Divil a one would dare venture out to meet a friend over a glass, or a girl at a dance, but instead was shut up at home not daring to raise a latch or draw the bolt, until the morning came.

On one such evening, after nightfall, Seamus was sitting around the fire, the only light in the room, with his mother and father waiting for the praties to boil and with noggins of buttermilk sitting ready for their supper. Suddenly there was a knock on the door.

'Whisht,' said the father, 'it's the soldiers come on us. Bad luck to them, the villains. I'm afraid they've seen a glimmer of the fire through the crack in the door.'

'No,' said the mother, 'for I'm after hangin' an ould sack and my new petticoat over the crack in the door.'

'Whisht anyway,' said the father, 'there's another knock.'

They all held their tongues until another thump was heard on door.

'Oh it's folly to pretend anymore,' said the father, 'they're too cute to put off. Go and see who it is Seamus.'

'How can I see who it is in the dark?' he demanded.

'Light the candle then and see who's in it but don't open the door for your life, barrin' they break it in,' said the father. 'Except to the soldiers if it's them and speak fair to them.'

Lighting the candle from the fire Seamus made his way nervously to the door.

'Who's there?' said Seamus.

'It's me,' said the voice on the other side.

'Who's me?' asked Seamus.

'A friend.'

'Baithershin!' said Seamus, 'who are you at all?'

'Arrah! don't you know me?'

'Divil a taste.'

'Sure it's Paddy the Piper that's in it,' said the voice on the other side of the door.

'Oh thunder and turf Paddy,' said Seamus, 'what brought you at this hour?'

'I didn't like goin' around by the road so I came the short cut and that's what delayed me,' said Paddy.

'Oh bloody wars,' said Seamus. 'I wouldn't be in your shoes Paddy, for the king's ransom, for you know it's a hangin' matter to caught out in these times.'

'Sure I know that, that's why I came to you to let me in for ould acquaintance sake,' said poor Paddy.

'Oh Paddy I daren't open the door for the wide world and sure you know it,' said Seamus. 'In truth if the Husshians or the Yeos catch you they'll murder you as sure as your name's Paddy.'

'Many thanks to you Seamus for your good intentions but I hope it's not the likes of that is in store for me. And faith then, more's the reason you should let me in.'

'It's a folly to talk 'cause I daren't open the door,' said Seamus.
'Well what will become of me at all, at all?' said Paddy.

'Get yourself to the shed behind the house where the cow
is,' said Seamus. 'There's a grand lock of straw for you to lie in.
It's a bed fit for a lord, let alone a piper.'

So without another word Paddy set off to find the shed in
the dark. Inside the house a sullen mood settled on the three
gathered around the fire. It wasn't in their hearts to turn him
away but with the times that were in it, they had little choice.
Their mood soured further when the praties were ready – for
the bit and the sup was always welcome to the poor traveller
under their roof.

When the praties were eaten and the buttermilk drunk the
family retired to bed, each with their own private thoughts
given over to poor Paddy in the shed. Each comforted themselves knowing that there was a good bed of straw and the
warmth of the cow. Paddy made himself comfortable in the
straw and was soon fast asleep, happy to be out of the road and
the soldiers.

How long he had been sleeping he didn't know, but Paddy
woke thinking it was morning. However, it was the light of a
big full moon that deceived him. He wanted to be stirrin' early
as there was a fair day in the town nearby. Paddy was hoping
to earn a few shillings for his piping and it has to be said that
there was divil a better piper in all around that country. Paddy
could play 'Jinny Bang'd the Weaver' beyond telling, and when
he opened up 'Hare in the Corn' you'd think the very dogs was
in it and the horsemen ridin' like mad.

Paddy set off for the fair and, as was his way, went meander-
ing through the fields. He hadn't gone far when he came to a
rise and had to climb up through a hedge. As he pushed his
head through he banged up against something that made the

fire flash out of his eyes. He steadied himself and took a closer look. Poor Paddy nearly fainted when his eyes fell on a corpse hanging from the branch of a tree.

'Good morning to you sir,' said Paddy, 'and is that the way with you my poor fellow? You took a start out of me for truth.'

It was a wonder that Paddy could be so calm for the sight would have made the heart of a stouter man jump to think of a Christian cratur hanging up like a dog. Now judging by the fact that the corpse still had clothes on, Paddy knew it was the 'boys', or rebels, who had hanged this chap. It was known that the soldiers never hanged anybody with good clothes on but only the poor and defenceless were left like this poor cratur.

'Well by my soul but they're a grand pair of boots,' said Paddy to the corpse, 'and here's me, the best piper for seven counties around, tramping about in this pair of auld brogues not worth three traneens. Sure wouldn't it make your soul happy to know your good boots were put to use being sported about the country by a fine fellow like myself.'

There was no answer to Paddy's question bar the sound of his own heavy breathing as he tried to remove the boots from the poor cratur hanging there. Whether it was that the boots were too tight or had become stiff, or because with the body dancing up and down on the branch, Paddy couldn't get a firm hold to gain an advantage. He gave up on his efforts and walked away. But glancing back he could see what a fine pair of boots they were and made up his mind to secure them, by means fair or foul!

That led Paddy to commit a foul and dirty deed, the only foul deed known to have been his. He pulled out a big knife with a fine buck handle and a murdering big blade. Now the knife had been given to Paddy by an uncle of Seamus's who was a gardener. Indeed it wasn't the first mischief it was responsible for, as it had cut the love between the two men who were the best of friends. It was a wonder to all that two such knowledge-able men, that ought to know better, would give and take sharp steel in friendship! Well Paddy swung the knife and what did he do but cut the legs clean off the poor cratur hanging there.

'I can take off the boots at my convenience,' said Paddy to himself and despite the awfulness of the dirty deed he thanked the corpse 'for your kindness'.

Paddy tucked the two legs under his arm to make his way towards the fair when the moon peeped out from behind a cloud.

'Oh! Is it there you are?' said he to the moon, for he was an impudent chap.

Realising his mistake in thinking it was the early morning, he was afraid for himself of being caught out and about by the soldiers and ending up like his friend that he had so mistreated. And bad as it was that he would be found tramping about at the hour, the nature of his baggage would certainly get him into extreme bother. He turned and made his way back to the safety and comfort of the cowshed. He hid the legs with his new boots in the straw and was soon asleep. And what do you think but the soldiers came along and found him in the shed. They took him away and many would say that it only served him right for his foul deed that night.

'Go to the shed Seamus and bid poor Paddy to come in and share the praties for I'm sure he's ready for his breakfast by now,' the father said when the morning came.

Seamus went out to the shed calling for Paddy. Getting no answer, he went inside to see could he raise his friend but there was still no answer from Paddy.

'Where are you hiding Paddy?' Seamus called, while search-ing the shed for some evidence of his presence. He spotted the two feet sticking out from under the straw.

'Well bad luck to you Paddy, haven't you made yourself as snug as a flea in a blanket,' said Seamus, 'but I'll shake you out of your dreams.'

With that Seamus made a grab at the two heels so as to drag Paddy from his comfort and dreams. What a shock he got when he found himself flying head over heels through the air and landed on the flat of his back. An even bigger shock awaited him when his vision cleared and he spied two things sticking out straight in front of him like two broom handles and realised that they were two mortal legs. He jumped to his own two feet and threw the legs to the ground.

'You murdering villain,' Seamus roared while shaking his fist at the cow. 'Oh you unnatural beast, you've eaten poor Paddy, you thievin' cannibal.'

Poor Seamus was beside himself.

'How dainty you are that nothing I serve you for your supper will do but the best piper in Ireland. Such foul murder! And what will the people say of such a thing?' said Seamus. 'And look at you all innocent looking munching on your hay as if nothing had happened.'

Seamus ran as fast as he could into the house. Not only did he want to tell his father but he was also nervous of being near the murdering beast.

'It ate Paddy you say?' said the father.

'Divil a doubt of it,' said Seamus.

'Are you sure?' asked the mother.

'I wish I was as sure of a new pair of brogues,' said Seamus. 'Bad luck to the bit she left of him but his two legs.'

'And did she eat the pipes too?' said the father.

'By gor I believe so.'

'Oh the devil fly away with her,' said the father. 'What a cruel taste in music she has.'

'Arrah don't be cursin' the cow that gives milk for the weans,' said the mother.

'Why shouldn't I curse such an unnatural beast?' asked he.

'You shouldn't curse any living thing under your own roof,' said the mother.

'By my soul then she shan't be under my roof for any longer,' declared the father. 'Take her into the fair this minute Seamus and sell her for whatever she'll get. Go off the minute you finish your breakfast.'

Seamus sat staring at the food in front of him. His appetite was gone. The fright of things in the shed and now the command of his father lay heavy on his brow.

'What's eating you now?' asked the father.

'In truth I'd rather not take that beast to the fair,' Seamus replied.

'Arrah don't be making a gom of yourself,' said he.

'Faith I'm not,' said Seamus.

'Well like it or no like it, you must drive her.'

'Sure father, you could take more care of her yourself.'

'That's mighty good,' said the father, 'to keep a dog and bark myself. (Seamus was to recollect that saying for many's the long year.) Let's have no more chat of it and be off with you.'

It was sore against poor Seamus to have to do with the villain. He cut a long wattle so he could drive the man-eater of a thief without being too near her. The road was mighty thronged with boys and girls, rich and poor, high and low, as it always was on a fair day.

'God save you,' said one to Seamus.

'God save you, kindly,' replied Seamus.

'That's a fine beast you're driving,' said he.

'Truth she is,' said Seamus, although in truth it went against his heart to have to say a good word about her.

'It's to the fair you're goin' with the beast I suppose,' said he. (He was a snug-looking farmer riding a pretty little grey hack.)

'Faith you're right there, tis the fair I'm headed to,' said Seamus.

'What do you expect for her then?' said he.

'Faith I don't know,' said Seamus and that was the truth of it. He was so bewildered about the whole thing.

'That's a quare way to be going to market,' said the farmer, 'not to know what to expect for the beast.'

'Och,' said Seamus, in a careless manner, trying not to arouse suspicion that there was anything wrong with her. 'Och sure, no one can tell what a beast will bring until they come to the fair and see what price is goin'.'

'That's true enough,' said he. 'But if you were bid a fair price before you come to the fair, sure you might as well take it.'

'Oh I've no objection,' said Seamus, anxious to be rid of the murderer.

'Well then, what will you ask for her?'

'Why I wouldn't like to be unreasonable so I'll take four pounds for her,' said Seamus, 'and no less.'

'No less!' said the farmer.

'Sure that's cheap enough.'

'In truth lad it's too cheap,' said the farmer, 'for if there wasn't something the matter, it's not for that price you'd be selling that fine milk cow, as she is in all appearance.'

'Indeed then upon my conscience she is a fine milk cow,' said Seamus.

'Maybe,' said he, 'she's gone off her milk in that she doesn't feel well?'

'Och by this and that,' said Seamus, 'in regard of feeding there's not the like of her in Ireland. So make your mind easy and if you like her for that money you may have her.'

'Why indeed I'm in no hurry and I'll wait to see how they go in the fair,' said he.

'You may well be disappointed,' said Seamus, pretending not to be concerned.

But in truth he was afraid people would see that there was something unnatural about her and that he'd never get rid of her at all, at all.

At last he came to the fair. What a great sight of people were there to greet him – you'd think the whole world was there. Along with the people were stalls selling gingerbread men, elegant ribbons and cloth for the making of beautiful gowns. There was pitch and toss and merry-go-rounds. Tents serving the best of drink and fiddles playing to encourage the boys and the girls. Seamus never minded a wit of it, so determined was he to be rid of his murdering beast. He drove the cow on into the thick of the fair when all of a sudden as he was passing a tent he heard the pipes struck up to the tune of 'Tattherin' Jack Welsh'. To his horror didn't the cow cock her ears and make a dart for the tent.

'Oh murder,' cried Seamus to the boys standing about, 'hold her, hold her. She ate one piper already and bad luck to her she wants another.'

'Is it the cow for to eat a piper?' said one of them.

'Devil a bit of lie, for I seen the corpse myself and nothing left but the two legs,' said Seamus. 'And it's folly to be trying to hide it for I see she'll never leave it now, as poor Paddy Grogan knows to his cost, Lord have mercy on him.'

'Who's that taking my name in vain?' came a shout from the crowd and with that the crowd moved aside as Paddy the Piper pushed his way through.

'Oh hold him too,' cried Seamus, 'Keep him off me for it's not himself God knows but his ghost, for he was killed last night to my certain knowledge.'

With that Paddy, for indeed it was him, fell about laughing so that those watching thought he was going to split his sides. When he came to himself again he said he needed a drink. They retired to a tent where it took a full gallon of spirits to explain the whole thing. Well you can imagine the *craic* that was had with that and poor Seamus had to take it all, doubting the poor cow and laying the blame for the eating of the piper on her. They drank to the health and long life of Paddy and the cow. Paddy played the pipes that day beyond all telling and many a one said the likes of it was never heard before or since, even from Paddy.

At the end of the day poor Seamus drove the slandered cow home again and she had many a quiet day after that. And when she died the father had her skinned and an elegant pair of breeches made out of the hide, such was the regard he had for her. And the breeches stayed in the family and Seamus wore them in his turn. And the queerest thing of all happened then, because from that out, when whoever was wearing those breeches heard the pipes start up a tune, they couldn't rest a minute but goes a jiggin' and jiggin' in their seat and never stops till the pipes stop.

18

THE BEE, THE HARP, THE MOUSE AND THE BUM-CLOCK

Once there was a widow who had just one son named Jack. They lived happy and well with their three cows that provided admirably for them. But alas hard times crept across the land and fell on Jack and his mother. The crops failed and hunger stared in the door. Things got bad for the widow and for want of money and for want of necessities she made up her mind to sell one of the precious cows.

'Go over to the fair in the morning Jack and sell the branny cow,' she said.

'Ah mother, are things so bad that we have to let the lovely cow go?' said Jack.

'They are, I'm sorry son, but you're not to worry your head. Just make sure you get a good price for that fine beast.'

In the morning the brave Jack was up early, had what little there was going for breakfast, took a stout stick and turned the cow onto the road. Jack marvelled at the multitude on the road heading to the fair. Soon he found himself surrounded by people and animals and enjoyed the merriment all around him. He observed the various cows on the road and looked favourably on his own branny cow that looked strong and healthy compared to some of the others.

Now when he entered the town he spied a great crowd gathered in a ring in the street. Curious, Jack made his way into the middle of the crowd. His eyes widened to saucers when he saw a man in the middle with a wee wee harp, a bee, a mouse and a bum-clock* in his hands. When the man put them all on the ground and whistled, the bee began to play the harp, and the mouse and the bum-clock stood up on their hind legs, took hold of each other and began to waltz with great elegance.

And as soon as the harp began to play and the mouse and bum-clock to dance, there wasn't a man or a woman that didn't begin to dance. Indeed everything in the fair, pots and pans, the wheels and reels, began to dance as well, jumping and jigging all over the town. And Jack and the branny cow were as bad as the next.

There was never a town in such a state before or since. After a while the man picked up the wee harp, the bee, the mouse and the bum-clock, and put them in his pocket. The men, the women, Jack and the cow, the pots and the pans, wheels and reels, that had hopped and jigged, came to a sudden stop. A great racket went up in the air as everyone began to laugh as if to break its heart.

As the crowd started to drift away the man turned to Jack.

'How would you like to be master of all these fine animals?' he asked.

'Why,' said Jack, 'I should like it fine.'

'Well then how will you and me make a bargain for them?'

'I have no money I'm afraid,' said Jack.

'But you have that fine cow,' the man replied. 'I will give you the bee and the harp for it.'

'Oh but my poor mother is at home with a terrible sadness and sorrow on her,' said Jack. 'And I have this cow to sell and lift her heart again.'

'And better than this she cannot get,' said the man. 'When she sees the bee play the wee harp she will laugh as if she never laughed in her life before.'

'Aye that she would and it would be grand to behold,' said Jack.

He made the bargain. The man took the branny cow and Jack started for home with the bee and the harp in his pocket. He was full of excitement and desiring to see that laugh on his mother's face he skipped home in jig time.

'Oh Jack, you're a sight for sore eyes,' said his mother in welcome. 'And I see you've sold the cow.'

'That I have mother,' said Jack.

'And did you do well?'

'Indeed I did and did very well mother,' said Jack.

'So how much did you get for her then?'

'Oh it wasn't money I got for her at all but something far better.'

'O Jack! Jack,' cried his mother, 'what have you done my son?'

'Just wait till you see mother, and you will say that I have done very well.'

Jack took the bee and the harp out of his pocket. His mother nearly fainted at the sight and was speechless. Jack set the bee and the harp on the ground, began to whistle and

the bee began to play the harp as
soon as he did. His mother let a
great laugh out of her and she and
Jack began to dance. The pots and pans, the
wheels and reels began to jig and dance over
the floor too and indeed the house itself hopped about also.
When Jack picked up the bee and the harp the dancing all
stopped and his mother laughed on for a long time. But when
she returned to herself her mood switched in jig time and a
dark cloud swept over her.

'Jack you're a foolish silly fellow,' she said with anger raging
across the room where laughter had danced only a short time
before.

'There's neither food nor money in the house and now we
have lost one of our good cows,' she said. 'You'll have to go to
the fair tomorrow and take the black cow to sell.'

Jack was up early and headed off to fair with his mother's warning to 'get a good price for her' ringing in his ears. He made his
way to the fair ignoring all the hustle and bustle on the road. But as
soon as entered the town he saw a big crowd in a ring in the street.

Said Jack to himself, 'I wonder what they are looking at?' his
curiosity ablaze.

He pushed himself into the crowd and saw the wee man
from the day before with a mouse and a bum-clock. He put
them down on the street and began to whistle. The mouse and
the bum-clock stood up on their hind legs and got hold of each
other and began to dance. As they did there wasn't a man or
woman in the street who didn't begin to jig also, and Jack and
the black cow, and the wheels and the reels, the pots and pans,
all of them were jigging and dancing all over the town. Indeed
the houses themselves were jumping and hopping about and
such a place Jack or any one else never saw before.

When the man lifted the mouse and the bum-clock they all stopped dancing and settled down, and everybody laughed heartily. The wee man turned to Jack again.

'I'm glad to see you again. And how would you like to have these animals?' asked he.

'I should like to have them very much only I cannot,' said Jack.

'And why is that Jack?'

'Oh I have no money,' said Jack, 'and my poor mother is very down-hearted. She sent me to the fair to sell this cow and to bring home some money to lift her heart.'

'Well if you want to lift your mother's heart I will sell you the mouse,' said the man. 'When you set the bee to play the harp and the mouse to dance to it, your mother will laugh as if she never laughed in her life before.'

'A kind offer indeed but as I say, I have no money sir to buy your mouse,' said Jack.

'Sure that is no issue Jack, I'll take your cow for it.'

Poor Jack was so taken with the mouse and had his mind so set on it, that he thought it was a grand bargain indeed. He gave the man the cow, took the mouse and started off for home. When he got home his mother welcomed him.

'You sold the cow Jack,' said she.

'I did that,' said he.

'Did you sell her well?'

'Very well indeed mother.'

'And how much did you get for her then?' asked his mother.

'Sure I didn't get money for her but great value I got,' said Jack.

'Oh Jack! Jack! Whatever do you mean?' she asked.

'I will show you that,' said Jack as he lifted the mouse out of his pocket, and the harp and the bee, and set the whole lot on the floor.

When Jack began to whistle the bee began to play, the mouse got up on his hind legs and began to dance and jig. Well Jack's mother gave such a hearty laugh as she never laughed in her life before. It made Jack's heart sing with delight to see such a sight and to know he had done the right thing. To dancing and jigging herself and Jack fell, the pots and the pans, the wheels and reels began to dance and jig all over the floor, and the house itself jigged too. And when they were tired of this Jack lifted the harp, the bee and the mouse and put them into his pocket. He delighted to watch his mother laugh for a long time. But when her laughter died away her mood changed in jig time and she got very down-hearted.

'You are a stupid, good-for-nothing fellow indeed,' said his mother. 'We have neither money nor meat in the house and here you have lost two of my good cows and now I only have the one left.'

She ordered Jack to take her last cow to the fair the next day and to make sure to bring home money to her 'to lift her heart'. He promised her he would and went to his bed with a stomach that growled as loud as the raucous in the house earlier.

Jack was up early and on the road to the fair with the spotty cow. When he arrived in the street he saw a crowd gathered in a ring. Of course Jack's curiosity wasn't going to allow him to walk on. He pushed his way into the crowd and there he saw the man he had seen on the two previous days. This time he held the bum-clock in his hand and he put it on the ground and started to whistle. As soon as he did the bum-clock started to dance and as before the men and women, the children in the street, Jack and the spotty cow all began to dance and jig along with the wheels and reels, the pots and the pans, and the houses themselves.

When the man lifted the bum-clock and put it in his pocket, everybody stopped their dancing and broke into a hearty laugh. The wee man turned and saw Jack.

'Well Jack my brave boy,' said the man, 'you will never be right fixed without the bum-clock, for it is a fancy thing to have.'

'Och but I have no money for such a thing,' said Jack.

'No matter for that, for you have a cow and that is as good to money to me,' he said.

'But I have a poor mother who is down-hearted at home and she sent me to the fair to sell this cow and raise some money to lift her heart.'

'Oh but Jack this bum-clock is the very thing to lift her heart, for when you put down the harp and the bee and mouse on the floor and put the bum-clock with them, she will laugh as if she never laughed in her life before.'

'Well that is surely true and I think I will swap with you,' said Jack.

So Jack gave the cow to the man and took the bum-clock himself and started for home. His mother was glad to see Jack home.

'I see you have sold the cow,' said she.

'That I did mother,' said Jack.

'And how much did you get for her?'

'Sure I didn't take any money for her mother but great value I did get for you,' said Jack.

With that he took out the wee harp, the bee, the mouse and the bum-clock, and set them on the floor. He began to whistle and the bee struck up the harp and the mouse and the bum-clock stood up on their hind legs and began to dance. Well Jack's mother laughed like she had never laughed before in all her living days. The wheels and the reels, the pots and the pans, went jigging and hopping over the floor and the house itself went jigging and hopping likewise. When Jack lifted up the animals and put them in his pocket, everything stopped and his mother laughed on for a long time after. But when she came to herself again and saw what Jack had done, a black anger descended on her.

'Now we're without money, food, or cow!' she thundered at him. She scolded him heartily, then sat down and began to cry.

Poor Jack, when he looked at himself he confessed that he was indeed a stupid fool entirely. He wondered to himself what he could do for his poor mother. He went out along the road thinking on what he could do when he met a wee woman who greeted him; 'Good-morrow to you Jack,' said she, 'and how is it you are not trying for the King of Ireland's daughter?'

'What do you mean?' asked Jack.

'Didn't you hear that the whole world has heard that the Kind of Ireland has a daughter who hasn't laughed for seven years and he has promised to give her hand in marriage, and give the kingdom along with her, to any man who will make her laugh three times.'

'If that is so,' said Jack, 'it is not here I should I be.'

Back to the house Jack went and gathered the bee, the harp, the mouse and the bum-clock. He put the lot in his pocket and headed for the road.

'And where are you off to now boy?' she asked.

'Mother it won't be long till you get news from me,' he said.

'Ah Jack what foolishness has gotten into you now?' she said.

'I told you I got value and value you will get,' said Jack and he said goodbye to her.

When he reached the castle there was a ring of spikes all around it with men's heads on nearly every spike. He didn't like the look of this and no mention of it had the wee woman made.

'Whose heads are these?' Jack asked one of the king's soldiers.

'Any man that comes here trying to win the king's daughter and fails to make her laugh three times, loses his head and has it exhibited on a spike,' said the soldier. 'These are the heads of the men that have failed so far.'

'A mighty big crowd,' noted Jack.

Then Jack sent word to tell the princess and the king that there was a new man who had come to win her hand. In a short time the king, the queen, the princess and the whole court came out and sat on grand chairs of gold and silver in front of the castle. Jack was ordered to come forward and undertake his trial.

Jack put his hand in his pocket and took out his menagerie and the harp. He gave the harp to the bee. He tied a string to one and the other, took the end of the string himself and walked into the castle yard with his animals behind him.

When the king and queen, and court saw poor ragged Jack with his bee and mouse and bum-clock hopping behind him on a string, they fell into a roaring of laughter that was loud and long. And when the princess lifted her head and looked to see what they were laughing at, saw Jack and his paraphernalia, she opened her mouth and let out such a laugh as never was heard before.

Jack dropped a low curtsey and said, 'Thank you my lady. I have one of the three parts of you won.'

Then he drew up his animals in a circle and began to whistle. The minute he did the bee began to play the harp, the mouse and bum-clock stood on their hind legs, took hold of each other and began to dance. With that the king, the queen, the court and ragged Jack himself began to dance and jig, and everything about the king's castle, pots and pans, wheels and reels and the castle itself began to dance.

The king's daughter, when she saw this, opened her mouth again and let out of her a laugh twice as loud as the one she let out before. And Jack in the middle of his jigging, dropped to a curtsey and said, 'Thank you my lady, that is two of the three parts of you won,' Jack and his menagerie went on playing and dancing but try as he did Jack couldn't get the third laugh out of the king's daughter. The poor fellow realised his big head was in danger of ending up on a spike.

Then the brave mouse came to Jack's help and wheeled round on its heel and as it did so its tail swiped into the bum-clock's mouth and the bum-clock started to cough and cough. When the princess saw this she opened her mouth again and let out the loudest, heartiest and merriest laugh yet.

'Thank you my lady,' said Jack dropping another curtsey, 'I have all of you won.'

Jack stopped his menagerie and the king took him and his animals into the castle. A clatter of servants descended on Jack, washed and combed him, and dressed him in a suit of silk and satin, with all kinds of gold and silver ornaments. He was then led before the princess. And true enough she confessed that a handsomer and finer fellow than Jack she had never seen and she was very willing to marry him.

Jack sent for his mother and she was brought along for the wedding which lasted for nine days and nights, every night better than the last. Each night Jack brought forth his menagerie and set the whole place to dancing.

Jack smiled at his mother and said, 'I told you they were value and value we have now.'

*A bum-clock is a Dor beetle.

19

GHOST LIGHTS IN RAMELTON

There was a woman who lived in Ramelton by the name of Aoife and if you had mentioned any of these events to her, she would have laughed. She was a religious woman and had no truck with superstitions or belief in anything other than God and mere mortals who walked the world like herself. She was a good Christian-living woman who didn't let alcohol pass her lips and tried to keep bad words about others firmly behind her. She went to church every day and was good to her neighbours.

Now her husband , Packie, was somewhat different in character. He led a good life, went to church every Sunday and was there to help his neighbours at the drop of the hat he kept firmly perched on his head, except when it rained. When asked why this was so, he promptly replied, 'Sure I wouldn't be sitting in the house with a wet cap on my head would I?'

Unlike his wife he was partial to a wee drop once in while and then his tongue was somewhat looser.

Despite his Christian values he was prone to a bit of poaching, especially in the river Lennon. Now you might think this was somehow contrary to his beliefs but in his view of the world he wondered 'how any man can claim to own a river when it is constantly flowing and moving from one place to another!'

Occasionally he would walk the fields in search of rabbits to vary the plate at home. His wife never commented on the fine salmon that he put on the table but her demeanour when rabbits were produced was somewhat different. Now this was not down to a different view of the rabbit over the salmon but more to do with the company he kept when out lamping.

These so called 'good boys' were fond of their messing about the town and even more fond of the poitín that was cooked up in the hills.

'Where are you off to at this hour?' Aoife asked him.

'Ah sure, I'm just going for a bit of a stroll with a few of the boys,' he said.

'Ha. A bit of a stroll indeed,' she snapped. 'Would this stroll involve Patsy or Johnny?'

'Aye, I think they'll be along,' he said.

'Well don't come back here drunk.'

On one such occasion the boys were up in the fields around Aughnagaddy House. They were out lamping for rabbits and as it was a clear night the temperatures had fallen so they had a wee drop to keep the chill off.

'We've being going around and around for ages,' complained Patsy some time later, 'and we've got nowhere.'

'I'm telling you the house was just over there,' said Johnny pointing.

'We've been over that way and it's not there,' said Patsy.

'I think we've been wandered, boys,' said Packie.

'Ah, don't be stupid man,' said Patsy and Johnny. 'You don't believe in that sort of nonsense.'

'Indeed I do. Many's the story I've heard of people been wandered by the good people,' said Packie.

'That's just the drop speaking,' said Patsy.

'Well how else can you explain the fact that we've been wandering around here like fools for God knows how long?' demanded Packie.

'We've just missed a gap in the hedge or something,' said Patsy.

'Well look at that branch there with my handkerchief on it,' said Packie. 'We've passed that branch four times now. We're just going around in circles.'

'What is your handkerchief doing there then?' said Johnny.

'I put it there when I thought we had been wandered,' said Packie.

'Ah you're just having us on with your handkerchief and wandering nonsense,' said Patsy.

'It's a fact and the best thing we can do is stop here till the good folk lift the wandering,' said Packie.

Just then they saw a light moving a short distance away.

'What's that?' said Patsy.

'I don't know,' said Packie, 'but will you look at the poor dog. It's frozen in terror and his hair is standing on end.'

'Quick, hide,' said Johnny.

The three of them fell to the ground and held the dog tight. They peered through the hedge as the light drew closer. There was no sound but they could see it was the window of a carriage on its way up to the house.

'That was close,' said Patsy.

'Ah, we must be closer to the house than we thought,' said Johnny.

'But why was the dog so scared?' asked Packie.

'He wasn't the only one,' said Patsy. 'You look like you saw a ghost.'

'Did you not feel it when that carriage went past?'

'Feel what?' said Johnny. 'And what carriage?'

'A terrible chill,' said Packie.

'And what carriage are you talking about?' said Johnny. 'I didn't hear the sound of any carriage.'

'Exactly. It was a ghost carriage I tell you,' said Packie.

'Ah don't be ridiculous. You've had too much to drink. First the wee folk wandering us and now ghosts,' said Johnny.

'I felt it too,' said Patsy.

'What?' said Johnny.

'Never mind your bravado Johnny,' said Patsy. 'I can see it in your eyes that you felt it too.'

'Well maybe there was something a bit odd about it,' said Johnny.

'I'm getting out of here,' said Packie. 'Look you can see the lights of the house now.'

The three friends headed away from the house and out onto the main road. As they stepped out they nearly crashed into Mickey.

'Where are you going like a crazy thing?' said Packie .

'It's yourself Packie,' said Mickey. 'I heard the sound of you coming and I thought it was that carriage coming back again.'

'What carriage?' said Patsy.

'I was coming down the road there on my bike when I see the two lights of a carriage coming up the road, a sight you don't see too often these days,' said Mickey. 'And because it's so dark I got off the bike and got into the side of the road. But the blasted thing came charging at me and knocked me into the ditch. It took me ages to crawl out of it with the bike on top of me.'

'How do you know it was a carriage?' Johnny asked him.

'I saw the lights,' said Mickey.

'We saw it too,' said Packie.

'We saw something,' said Patsy. 'But we didn't hear anything.'

'It was that carriage,' said Packie. 'We saw the light from within but it weren't a natural thing I tell you.'

They all headed down the brae towards the town. The first house they came to was Packie's.

'Don't be annoying that wife of yours with your stories,' Patsy warned.

'Sure she won't believe a word of it anyway,' said Packie.

He went inside to be greeted by a suspicious-looking Aoife.

'You're home early and not a rabbit in sight,' she began, but stopped when she saw his face. 'Good God, what happened?' she said. 'You look like you've seen a ghost.'

And with that he told the whole of the curious incidents of the night.

'Too much drink, that's what it is,' Aoife declared.

'And what about Mickey,' said Packie. 'Your own cousin and him coming home from work.'

'Ah, he's always imagining things in the dark,' she said.

'It's true I'm telling you Aoife.'

'Aye, true like that story you told me about the fish earlier today,' she said.

'That was the truth.'

'You expect me to believe that a salmon knocked Patsy out cold and then flapped back into the river.'

'Well where else did it go?' he asked.

'The fool let it go.'

'He did not,' said Packie. 'I thought I saw the keeper just after we hauled it in. It was huge. I said 'run'. I went one way and when I looked back Patsy was struggling to his feet with the fish. I went and hid myself and waited. I didn't see any sign of the keeper and guessed I must have imagined it so I went back to find Patsy. And there he was lying flat on his back where I had seen him last but no fish. He had a right bump on the side of his face.'

'Ah, get out of it you with your auld stories,' said Aoife.

Now about a week later Aoife was coming out of church after evening mass when she met her friend Maggie.

'Do you fancy a wee walk Aoife?' said Maggie. 'It's such a lovely night.'

'Aye I would,' said Aoife. 'I'm in no hurry home as Packie is out with the boyos.'

They headed up along the Letterkenny Road. They chatted away as they walked with nothing to disturb the night other than the hoot of an owl.

But suddenly they both cried out and stood stock still. They felt a terrible chill creeping over them. Then they saw it, two carriage lights approaching at great speed. They knew they should step in to let it pass but they were frozen to the spot in terror. Then the two lights came on top of them and passed on through. Neither of them could speak nor move for some time.

'What was that?' whispered Maggie at last.

'I don't believe I'm saying this but I think it was a ghost carriage,' said Aoife. 'I laughed at poor Packie when he told me they had seen something like it last week.'

The two women turned on their heels and headed home. By the time they arrived Packie was sitting in his chair by the fire.

'What's happened to you?' he asked. 'You look like you've seen a ghost.'

'Well God forgive me for not believing you last week,' said Aoife. 'But I wouldn't have believed it if I hadn't seen it with my own two God-given eyes.'

And from that day on she wasn't as quick to dismiss Packie's stories, but she rarely spoke of what she herself had witnessed that night.

20

THE STRANGE MASS

There was a young lad who lived just outside Ramelton years ago, who was known to all in the area. The boy was not known for any mischief or wrong doing but instead for his friendly nature, his curiosity and his good Christian living. He served on the altar at Mass and helped the priest out in any way he could. The boy also loved stories and was to be found at any house where there was telling. He would hide himself under the table of any kitchen where there was raking and he would fill his head with wild imaginings spurred on by the tales.

He would often come home and regale the household with some of the stories he heard. Although it must be said that there were many he didn't repeat under his own roof for he knew his mother was of a delicate disposition. Of course his mother, and indeed the priest, would chastise him even for the innocent stories he told them, telling him not to be believing in such 'foolish superstition'. Now the lad saw no harm in the stories and was equally keen to listen to the stories of the Bible.

One day when he came home with the tale of Mrs Patton from the Brae. She was sitting near the back of the church when she fell fast asleep. It wasn't long before the poor woman started farting in the seat. You can imagine the sniggering it set off around her. The good boys at the back were having great gas out of it but one of them, who was a neighbour of hers, felt sorry for her. He tapped her on the shoulder: 'Mrs Patton, your back door is open,' he said.

'Oh the chickens will get in and eat all the corn,' she said as she jumped up and ran out of the church.

Of course this got a great laugh all together.

Now the priest had his back to the congregation and saw nothing of the goings on but the lad's ear had caught the sniggers and managed to glimpse Mrs Patton rushing out of the church. He got all the details from the good boys after Mass.

His mother was horrified at his tale. 'Don't use that sort of language in this house dear – it's unbecoming,' she said, 'and don't be telling tales like that. It's unchristian.'

In fairness to the boy he said nothing to the priest about it for he didn't want to embarrass Mrs Patton. However, there was another story he recounted to the priest and he regretted it greatly. In fact the priest's face lit up like the fire and the boy was afraid he was going to cuff him.

'Father did you hear about that woman over in Milford who saw the ghost in the church?'

'I've told you before, there's no such things as ghosts,' the priest said.

'But Father this woman is a good Christian, she goes to Mass everyday and then to the church in the evening to say the Rosary,' the boy said.

'And what has that got to do with it?'

'Well you can believe a woman like that Father,' the boy said.

'Hmm. And what was it she was supposed to have seen?'

'Well Father, she was in the church like I said, saying her Rosary. It was evening time and there was no one else there.

All of sudden she heard movement at the front of the church and there on the altar she saw a priest who looked awful familiar all in his vestments.'

'There's nothing unusual about that,' said the priest.

'Ah but Father there's no Mass at that time though.'

'Maybe he was saying a special Mass for some reason,' said the priest.

'Oh it was a special mass alright for the priest turned around and asked 'is there anyone here to answer my Mass?' Well the woman was about to say yes but when she looked closely she saw that the priest was the parish priest who had died the week before. She didn't hang around I can tell but ran for her life,' said the boy.

'What utter nonsense and how dare you tell such lies,' the priest boomed, his face all aglow. He stepped towards the boy who cowered out of fear. The priest took a strong hold of his arm and shook him.

'That man was a friend of mine, a good and holy man who lived his life in the service of God. I will not allow such stories to be told about him.'

The boy had never seen the priest angry like this and he had seen him angry many times. When he pushed the boy towards the door he took to his heels for home and said nothing to his mother.

On occasion the boy and his mother would walk out to the church at Killycreen, for relatives of hers were buried there. On one such evening the night crept in fast and light dimmed in the church. Now the boy was sitting next to the wall and whether it was the fading light or the fact he had been out late the night before listening to stories, he fell asleep. When the Mass ended people made their way out and home. Because it was dark his mother assumed that the boy was walking with some of his friends and so set off home.

Now how long he had been asleep the boy didn't know but he was awoken by the sound of a bell. He looked up to see the altar bathed in the bright light of candles. He was surprised to see the place empty. The priest turned and asked, 'Is there anyone to serve the Mass?'

'I will Father,' said the boy.

He joined the priest on the altar and carried out all his usual tasks with reverence, answering all the prayers in turn.

When the Mass ended the priest turned to him. 'Thank you for serving my Mass. You have set me at peace with this world and the next,' the priest said.

The boy didn't know what he was talking about but as he walked out of the church he glanced back. It was in complete darkness where it had been bathed in light before he turned his head. He felt a chill run down his spine.

He glanced out across the graveyard and he thought he saw a shape moving through the graves. He followed it to the spot where it disappeared from sight. In the light of the moon it saw it was the grave of a priest who had died some time in the past. He realised then that he had served a Mass for the ghostly priest. He hadn't recognised the priest but then he hadn't come to that church too often.

When he got home his mother lit on him.

'Where have you been? I've been awful worried about you.'

'Ah, I was just chatting with a few of the lads,' he said, saying nothing of his encounter.

He did mention it the next night though, when he went to a house to listen to stories. They all listened, rapt in his tale.

'I had heard some stories of strange lights up at that church,' said the man of the house.

But there were never any reports of strange lights again and the boy was delighted to tell his story whenever he could, but he never mentioned it to his mother or the priest.

21

THE OLD HAG OF THE FOREST

Once upon a time, long long ago, when there were more kings and queens in Ireland than windows in O'Donnell's old castle, and when witches and enchantments were as plentiful as blackthorn bushes, there were a king and queen who had three sons. To each of these sons the queen had given a hound, a hawk and a horse. The horse could overtake anything. The hound could catch anything it pursued on dry land and the hawk could take anything in the air or in the water.

In time the three boys had grown up to be fine, able, strapping young men and the oldest decided to go out into the world and make his fortune.

'And why do you want to do that?' asked the king and queen, who were fond of their sons. They pleaded with him not to go but to no avail.

'My time has come,' he said. 'I cannot hang on the generosity of my parents forever. Now give me your blessing and I'll be on my way.'

The king and the queen gave their son their blessing and he mounted his horse, with his hawk on his shoulder and the hound at his heels and prepared to leave.

'Watch each day the water that settles in the hoof tracks outside the gate,' he said. 'As long as the water keeps clear I'm alright, but when you see it frothing I'm fighting a hard battle and if you ever see it turn bloody I'm either dead or under an enchantment.'

And so he took his leave and headed off on his horse with the hawk and the hound. He travelled far, far away from the castle, over many miles and many days until at last he came in sight of a great castle. When he saw the castle he pulled up his horse and looked about. In the distance he spied a wee house and made his way to it. Inside he found an old woman in what was a very neat and clean little house.

'God save you, young gentleman,' said the woman.

'God save yourself kindly and thank you,' said the lad. 'And can I have lodging for the night for myself, my hawk, my hound and my horse?'

'Well for yourself you can,' said the old woman, 'but I don't like them animals but sure you can house them outside.'

The young man agreed, settled the animals outside and made himself comfortable in the house in front of the fire. He was weary from his travels and was beginning to dose in front of the warm flames when the old woman asked him, 'I suppose you're here for the big fight tomorrow?'

'What big fight is this then?' said the lad.

'Och sure, the king's daughter of the castle beyond is to be killed by a great giant tomorrow unless there is a man who will fight him and beat him,' she said. 'If he does the king will give his daughter in marriage and the weight of herself three times in gold.'

'Och,' said he, 'I'll not go near it. I'll find something better to do with myself, maybe a spot of hunting.'

The next morning he was up early and pretended he was off hunting but went instead to the king's castle. There was no end of a crowd gathered there, brought in by the four winds of the world. Some of them were thinking of fighting the giant so as to win the king's daughter but most were there to look on out of curiosity. However, when the giant appeared, not a man of all the warriors gathered, and they covered all over in coats of iron mail from the crown of their heads to the soles of their feet, stepped forward. They trembled with fear for they had never seen such a giant, or even heard tell of one, in their lives. The king's son waited till he saw that none present would venture to fight and then he stepped out himself.

The giant and he went to it and the like of it was never before witnessed in Ireland. Backwards and forward they went, landing blows, defending and dodging out of the way of other blows. They were well matched in all but cunning and eventually the king's son saw his chance, leaped into the air and came down with his sword just right on the giant's neck. He cut the head clean off the giant. But he didn't wait around but slipped away into the crowd and disappeared. He went to the hills where he killed some game, came back to old woman's cottage and gave her the game for supper.

That night when she gave him supper the old woman told him about the great hero that had killed the giant that day and then disappeared.

'But the giant's brother is to be there tomorrow to fight anyone willing to fight for the king's daughter,' she said. 'You should go; it will be worth seeing.'

'Och, I'll find something more worthwhile to do with myself. I'll not go near it,' he said.

The next morning he was up early again and pretended to go off hunting but again made his way to the castle. Well the crowd was even bigger than before as news of the sport from the previous day had spread. When the giant appeared he was twice as impressive as the first and no man had the heart to venture to fight. At last the brave king's son stepped out again for the encounter.

Well, if the fight the day before was hard, it was twice as hard this day. Backwards and forwards they went, landing blows, defending and dodging out of the way of other blows, all double the day before's efforts. They were well matched in all but cunning and the king's son saw his chance again, leaped into the air and came down with his sword just right on the giant's neck. He cut the head clean off the giant. But he didn't wait around but slipped away into the crowd and again disappeared. He went to the hills to hunt, came back to the old woman's cottage and gave her the game for supper.

When the old woman was giving him his supper she told him all about the events of the day and the king's son hardly recognised the events that he had been so intimately involved in, such was the wonder of her tale. And she told him that another giant was to appear the next day to kill the king's daughter.

'It will be a wonderful day entirely, you should surely go to view the spectacle,' she said.

'Och, I'll find something better to fill my day with than that,' he said. 'I'll not go near it to look at him or it but go hunting instead.'

On the third morning he was up and away early, again pretending to go off hunting. When the third giant appeared people could see that he was even more magnificent and horrible than the other two put together. Again the brave lad set to with the giant and the fighting was even more odious than the previous two days combined. But the short and the long of it is, he leapt into the air and coming down on the giant's neck cut his head clean off. As before he disappeared into the crowd but lo and behold as he was disappearing, didn't one of the king's soldiers snap the shoe off his foot. So home he had to go that night with one shoe missing.

For days after the king had all his men out scouring the countryside far and wide to see if they could find the owner of the shoe. Thousands flocked to the castle but not one of them would the shoe fit. And on each of these days the lad was out hunting in the hills with his hawk, his hound and his filly. At last the old woman went to the castle and told the king how she had a lodger who came home the night the last giant was killed with only one shoe.

The next day the king came himself, with a carriage and four horses, and took the lad away to the castle. The king placed the shoe on the foot of the brave lad and it fitted like it had been made on his foot. The wedding was organised and a grander event hadn't been seen in many the long year. The whole gentry and nobility of all the land were invited to the great feast.

But lo and behold, when the celebrations were at their height in the ballroom and all were busy as bees in the kitchen, what should come sneaking up to the kitchen window but a hare. The hare put its head in through the window and started licking a plate of a particularly delicious and dainty dish that was cooling. When the cook saw this she was so enraged at one of her very best dishes being destroyed that she exploded.

'Well this is a nice how do you do with a hero in the house that killed three giants and a dirty hare is allowed come in and spoil my cooking,' she roared.

Word of this soon came to the groom's ear in the ballroom and though the king and the queen and his bride and all the nobility and gentry tried to persuade him against it, he declared that 'I won't sleep two nights in the same bed till I catch that hare and bring it back dead or alive.'

So mounting his filly, taking with him his hawk and his hound, he started off in hot pursuit. He pursued the hare all that night and all the next day and as evening drew in he spotted a wee house in a hollow. Feeling tired he went into the empty house, determined to rest for the night. He wasn't long in warming himself at the fire, with his hound, his hawk and his filly, when he heard a noise at the wee window of the house. When he looked up he saw a dirty wizened old hag of a woman, trembling and shaking to her very finger tips.

'Och, och, och it's cold, cold, cold,' said she with the teeth rattling in her head.

'Why don't you come in and warm yourself?' said he.

'Och, I can't. I can't,' said she. 'I'm afraid of them wild animals of yours. But here,' said she, pulling three long hairs out of her head and handing them in by the window to him, 'here's three of the borochs* we used to have in olden days and if you tie them wild beasts of yours with them, I'll go in.'

So he took the three hairs and tied the hawk, the hound and the filly. Then the old hag went in but she was trembling no longer and her eyes flashed red with fire.

'Do you know who I am?' she asked. 'They call me the Old Hag of the Forest and it was my three sons you killed to win the king's daughter, but you'll pay dearly for it now.'

With that she drew a sword and the lad drew his and they fell to it in the little house. It was a terrible fight and left the three battles with the giants look like play acting in comparison. But the Hag of the Forest was getting the upper hand and he had to call the hound.

'Hound, hound,' he cried, 'where are you at my command?'

'Hair, hair,' said the hag cried, 'hold tight.'

'Oh,' said the hound, 'it's hard for me to do anything and my throat a-cutting,'

'Hawk, hawk,' he cried, 'where are you at my command?'

'Hair, hair,' cried the old hag, 'hold tight.'

'Oh,' said the hawk, 'sure it's hard to me to do anything and my throat a-cutting.'

'Filly, filly,' he cried, 'where are you at my command?'

'Hair, hair,' cried the old hag, 'hold tight.'

'Oh,' said the filly, 'sure it's hard for me to do anything and my throat a-cutting.'

Overcoming our hero, the old hag took out of her pocket a little white rod; she struck him with it and turned him into a grey rock just outside the door. Then striking the hound, the hawk, and the filly with the rod she turned them into white rocks beside him.

Now at home his family watched the water in the filly's hoof tracks till at last one day they watched the water frothing and they said he was fighting a hard battle, and so he was that very day fighting the first giant. The next day it was frothing more than ever, for that was the day he was fighting the second giant and on the third day the water frothed right up out of the tracks. Then they knew he was fighting a desperate big battle entirely. The water settled and they were all greatly relieved. But at length didn't they find the water turning to blood and they thought he must be killed.

So the next morning the second brother set out and said he wouldn't sleep two nights in the one bed or eat two meals of meat in the one house till he found out what had happened to his brother. He took his hound, his hawk and his filly with him and he travelled far, far away from the castle, over many miles and many days until at last he came in sight of a wee house near a great castle where his brother had put up before him. When he went into the house the old woman flew at him and kissed him and welcomed him back with a hundred welcomes ten times over, for he was so like his brother she was sure it was him.

'They are all waiting for you anxiously at the castle,' she said. 'You must lose no time going to them as they're expecting you back every day and your bride is particularly down-hearted thinking that she'll never see you again.'

He started at once for the castle and he was greeted by great rejoicing and the pretty king's daughter covered him all over with kisses. There was a great feast with all the gentry and nobility invited again. And lo and behold didn't the hare come a second time and spoil the cook's best dish and drove her into a frightful rage.

'It's a nice how do you do indeed with a hero in the house that slew three giants, a hare would be allowed to come in and spoil my choicest dish, and then go off with itself scot free.'

And this word came to the new groom in the ballroom.

'By this and by that,' he said, 'I won't stop till I go after that hare, and I'll never stop two nights or eat two meals in the one house until I bring back that hare dead or alive.

And so off he starts with his hound, his hawk and his filly and pursued the hare all that night and the next day. Late the next evening when he was feeling tired out and not able to follow any further he spotted a wee house in a hollow and feeling tired he went in, determined to rest for the night. He wasn't long in warming himself at the fire, with his hound, his hawk and his filly, when he sees an old hag quaking and shaking all over.

'Och, och, och it's cold, cold, cold,' said she, trembling all over.

'Why don't you come in and warm yourself?' he asked.

'Oh,' said she, 'I can't go in for I'm afraid of them wild animals of yours.' Taking three hairs from her long hair she adds, 'here's three of the kind of borochs we used to use long ago. Tie your animals with them and then I'll go in.'

So he took the hairs and tied the hound, the hawk and the filly with them and then the old hag came in and not trembling at all now her eyes flashed fire and she said; 'Your brother killed my three sons and I have made him pay dearly for it and I'll make you pay dearly too.'

With that she drew a sword, as did he, and they fought long and hard until the hag was getting the better of him.

'Hound, hound,' he cried, 'where are you at my command?'

'Hair, hair,' cried the hag, 'hold tight.'

'Oh,' said the hound, 'it's hard for me to do anything and my throat a-cutting,'

'Hawk, hawk,' he cried, 'where are you at my command?'

'Hair, hair,' cried the old hag, 'hold tight.'

'Oh,' said the hawk, 'sure it's hard to me to do anything and my throat a-cutting.'

'Filly, filly,' he cried, 'where are you at my command?'

'Hair, hair,' cried the old hag, 'hold tight.'

'Oh,' said the filly, 'sure it's hard for me to do anything and my throat a-cutting.'

In the end of it all the hag got the better of him and took out a little white rod out of her pocket and struck him with it, turning him into another grey stone outside the door. Then she struck the hound, the hawk and the filly, and turned the three into white stones just beside him.

Now at home as before they were watching the filly's foot tracks everyday as regular. All was well until at length one day they saw the water turn bloody and then they were afraid that he was dead. The next morning the youngest son Jack said, 'I'll start off with my hound, my hawk and my filly, and won't sleep two nights in one bed or eat two meals in the one house till I find what has happened to my two older brothers.'

Jack took his hound, his hawk and his filly with him and he travelled far, far away from the castle, over many miles and many days until at last he came in sight of a wee house near a great castle where his two brothers had put up before him. When he went into the house the old woman flew at him and kissed him and welcomed him back with a hundred thousand welcomes.

'It is a poor thing for you to go away and leave your bride twice,' she said. 'She's in a bad way, down-hearted entirely and wondering what has become of you.'

She hurried the brave Jack off to the castle. And what a welcome awaited him there. And just like before a great feast was called for, and the gentry and nobility were all asked to it. And at the height of the fun word came to the ballroom about that unmannerly hare spoiling the cook's best dish. Again the cook flew into a fury at such a thing when there was a hero in the house that slew three giants.

With that Jack insisted on starting out in pursuit and there was no holding him for he was bound to fetch back that hare, dead or alive. And so off Jack starts with his hound, his hawk and his filly and pursued the hare but he had a notion that this same hare was nothing good and that was what had led his brothers astray, whatever had happened to them. He travelled all that night and the next day, and late the next evening when he was feeling tired out, he spotted a wee house in a hollow that his brothers had visited before. He wasn't long inside warming himself at the fire, with his hound, his hawk and his filly, when he heard a noise at the window and there he saw the old hag trembling, quaking and shaking all over.

'Och, och, och it's cold, cold, cold,' said she.

'Come in and warm yourself at the fire,' said Jack.

'Och,' she said, 'I'm afraid of those wild animals of yours.'
Taking three hairs from her long hair she adds, 'here's three of
the kind of borochs we used to use long ago. Tie your animals
with them and then I'll go in.'

Jack took the three hairs and, pretending to tie the hound,
the hawk and the filly with them, he threw them in the fire
instead. The old hag came in with her eyes blazing in her head
and drawing a sword she rushed at Jack. He drew his sword and
the two went at it hard and fast. Jack was struggling to stay the
course with her.

'Hound, hound,' he cried, 'where are you at my command?'

'Hair, hair,' cried the hag, 'hold tight.'

'Oh,' said the hair, 'it's hard for me to do good and me burning in the fire.'

'Hawk, hawk,' he cried, 'where are you at my command?'

'Hair, hair,' cried the old hag, 'hold tight.'

'Oh,' said the hair, 'sure it's hard for me to do good and me
burning in the fire.'

'Filly, filly,' he cried, 'where are you at my command?'

'Hair, hair,' cried the old hag, 'hold tight.'

'Oh,' said the hair, 'sure it's hard for me to do good and me
burning in the fire.'

So the hound, the hawk and the filly all rallied to Jack's aid.
The hound got hold of the hag by the heel and wouldn't let
go of her. With one fling the filly broke her leg and the hawk
picked out her two eyes, so she couldn't see what she was doing,
or where she was striking. She cried out: 'Mercy, mercy, spare
my life,' she said, 'and I'll give you back your brothers.'

'All right,' said Jack, 'tell me where they are and how I'm to
get them.'

'Do you see them two grey stones outside the door,' she said,
'with three smaller white ones around each of them?'

'I do,' said Jack.

'The grey stones are your brothers and the others are their hounds, their hawks and their fillies. If you take water from the well at the foot of that tree below the house and sprinkle three drops on each of the stones, they'll all be disenchanted.'

Jack didn't lose any time doing this and lo and behold, the stones came to life showing his two brothers, their hounds, their hawks, and their fillies, just the same as they were before the enchantment by the Old Hag of the Forest. Jack rejoiced to see his brothers that he had feared he would never see again.

Soon they were away with their hounds, their hawks and fillies, away for the castle again. There was great celebration on their return and the eldest brother got his bride. A grand feast was spread again and all the gentry and nobility of both that and the surrounding countries all came to attend and do honour to the bride and groom. Such a time of eating, drinking, dancing, singing, fun and amusement was never seen before or after.

Jack and the second brother started away off afterwards for home with their hounds, their hawks and their fillies and as much gold as they could carry.

*The boroch is the rope used in tying a cow to a stake.

22

STUMPY'S BRAE

There once lived a pedlar who travelled wide and far to sell his goods. He was known as Tom the Toiler, such was the work he did and the large pack he carried full of his wares. He sold all sorts of things to bring delight to families; ribbons to beautify a dress, cloth for the making of gowns, trinkets of all sizes and colours and practical items to make life that bit easier in the home.

Now Tom was known by all as a kind, hard-working man. He never had an ill word to say of anyone or anything. As well as his wares he would bring news from other places and sometimes the odd story. He was always made welcome in any house where he sought lodgings wherever that may be and indeed at whatever hour it may be. He was always willing to pay, for his purse was always full, but more often than not people refused such was the generosity of his company. When times were hard, or if Tom saw the family was struggling, he was sure to leave a coin for them.

Well, one night Tom was making his way from Lifford along the road towards Letterkenny. There had been a fair day in Strabane and he had done a swift business. His pack was light and his purse heavy. So good was the day that Tom had allowed himself to dally a while and enjoy a drink.

As he walked the road he was a happy and contented man with the company of the harvest moon and the quiet of the stars. His path was clear and all around draped in the soft moonlight. It was a still night and the sound of the river flowing was soothing to his ears. He was growing tired though and hungry and decided to rest for the night soon rather than make it further on towards Letterkenny. As he came down the steep brae from Lifford to Craighadoes he spied a light in the window of a cottage.

Now inside the cottage sat an elderly couple. They too had been to the fair but their day had been very different. They had sold a few animals but the price they got was poor.

'Oh good God, but what are we going to do?' asked the wife. 'Those few coins are not going to do us any good.'

'I don't know do I?' the husband said. 'If we don't get more of these soon,' shaking the coins in his hand, 'we'll be out on the side of the road.'

'You should never...' the woman started but the man cut her short.

'Whisht now with that. We were both agreed.'

They fell silent, staring into the fire with their own private thoughts. However, they were soon roused from their reverie by a gentle tapping on the door.

'Who is it at this hour?' called the man.

'I'm a pedlar looking for shelter for the night,' he said. 'You may have heard of me as some people call me Tom the Toiler. I can pay my way.'

Well, with that their eyes lit up. The man went to the door and lifted the latch.

'Come in, come in; you're welcome,' they said.

'God's blessing on the house and all who live beneath her,' said Tom, dropping his large pack on the ground where it landed with a gentle thud.

'You're travelling light tonight,' said the woman.

'Aye indeed, for it was busy day in Strabane today and thank the Lord but it is my purse that is heavy tonight,' said Tom. Now Tom knew these parts well and knew the people to be kind, God-fearing people.

'Aye it was a busy day indeed in Strabane,' said the man. 'We had a few beasts to sell but not a great price to be had.'

'I heard that too,' said Tom. 'Many a man was grumbling this evening.'

Well, after eating and chatting on for a while Tom said that he had an early start and should get to bed. The man showed him through to a small room off the fire with a bed.

'Good night to you both and God bless your generosity,' said Tom.

'God Bless your own generosity too,' said the woman, for Tom had paid over his coin, as he would leave early in the morning.

The couple sat on by the fire for some time. When all sound had settled in the room the woman whispered to her husband.

'Did you see the coins in his purse?'

'Indeed I did. Didn't I see him at the fair and the throngs around him buying his useless bits and bobs,' he said. 'No wonder there was poor money for the beasts when the women were spending their money with him.' He spat bitterly into the fire.

It was at this point that a voice began to whisper in his ear. They were church-going people as was the norm but the voice was not one that would be heard there. In fact, it was one that was regularly condemned for it was the voice of the devil. It took hold and the thoughts formed in the man's head.

'We could do away with him inside and take his purse, that would solve our problems,' said the man, casting a wicked stare towards his wife.

'Why I was thinking the same myself,' said the woman who was no better than him. 'What use does he have for it and we in dire need?'

The man rose from his seat as quiet as a mouse and grabbed his pick that lay against the wall inside the front door. He crept to the room where the pedlar was sleeping and pushed in the door. The pedlar stirred in his bed but that was the last of his movement for the man murdered him with his pick.

'What will we do with the body now?' said he to his wife.

'We can bury him in his own pack,' said she. 'I've emptied out the few bits in it and we can be at the loss of the pack.'

'Indeed we'll be better off without,' said he.

Between them they dragged the unfortunate pedlar from the room and stuffed him into the pack.

'Well damn him,' said the woman, 'and his long legs.'

He was too big for the pack, despite its size.

'What will we do?' said the man.

'You're a doting silly ould man,' said she, 'sure just knick him off at the knee.'

They took his legs off at the knee and packed the whole lot tightly into the pack. They carried the pack out into the moonlit night and made their way over the burn to dig a hole in the roots of a tree to bury the shortened pedlar. They threw the pack into the hole with the pedlar lying on his back. Well such a shock they got when the pedlar sat up and said:

'A right pair are ye thinking you'd lay me snugly here where none should know my station. But I'll haunt ye far, and I'll haunt ye near, father and son, with terror and fear, to the nine-teenth generation.'

The couple filled in the grave and crossed the burn back to their house. Despite the night they had and the prediction of the pedlar they both slept soundly that night, knowing their money worries were at an end.

The two were sitting the next night by the fire at the same hour as their murderous deed when the wee dog started to cower and whimper. The flames began to dance with a blue light and they knew that evil was afoot. There came a knock to the door and a heavy, heavy tread. The sound was terrifying and unnatural. It was the sound of a man stumping over the ground on the bare bones of his knees.

'May God forgive us,' cried the woman but to no effect.

In through the door he came like a breath of air, stump, stump, stump around the room he went with his bloody head and his knee bones bare.

The next morning the woman's black locks were as white as the snow on the mountains. And the man, who had stood as straight as a staff the night before, rose in the morning bowed like a rush in the wind.

Each and every night as the hour approached, the dog would cower and whimper and the fire tinge with blue. The terrible sound of the stump, stump, stump would fill the air and through the door he would drift.

One night after three days of rain and the burn roaring in fury, the wife looked at her husband sitting by the fire.

'Don't look so pale this night for the stumpy will not be here tonight. He cannot cross the burn in that for the water is up to the Jinn, over the back and up to the ridge of the meadow.'

But her soothing words had little effect as the stumpy came harplin' in and gave the wife a slap on the chin.

'Sure I came round by the bridge,' said he and stump, stump, stump away he went over stools and chairs; the sound of ten men and women dancing pairs was there.

No more could they take. They sold up and boarded a ship for America.

But sure who can flee their appointed punishment? As the eastern wind helped the ship glide through the ocean, what was the first sound that fell on their ears on the wide smooth deck? Aye you guessed it, the tapping of those bare knees. They made their weary way out to the woods in America but stumpy was there before them and haunted them till their dying day. And true to his word he continued to haunt their children down the years.

And if you happen to be passing by the place of this terrible deed and you should see a man stumping about on the bones of his knees sure you'll know it is Stumpy himself.

23

GRACE CONNOR – A GHOST STORY

Thady and Grace Connor lived in a tiny cabin on the borders of a large bog in the parish of Clondevaddock on the Fanad peninsula where they could hear the great Atlantic surge and thunder on the shores and watch the wild storms of winter sweep in over Muckish Mountain and his rugged neighbours. Even on the brightest summer's day the little cabin was dull and dreary with smoke filling the air.

While Thady did his best to eke a living from the small patch of land, growing what he could, Grace made a livelihood as a pedlar. She would carry a basket of remnants of cloth, calico, drugget and frieze about the country. The people round about rarely visited any large town and found it convenient to buy from Grace who was welcomed in many a local house where a table was hastily cleared so that she might display her wares. Being considered a very honest woman, people often entrusted her with errands to the shops in Letterkenny and Ramelton. As she set out to return to her own home her basket was generally laden with food for her children.

'Grace dear,' one of the kind housewives would say, 'here's a farrel of oaten cake with a wee scrape of butter for the weans.'

'Here's half a dozen of eggs dear,' another would say, 'you've a big family to support.'

When she arrived home her weans of all ages would gather round her to see what gifts were in the basket. With her honesty and thrift she managed to keep hunger from the door of their small cabin. But illness fell heavy on Grace Connor and she passed away. The family were devastated and none so more than Thady. She was waked as handsomely as he could afford and people came from wide and far to offer their condolences.

The night after the funeral Thady lay in his bed with the fire still burning brightly and his heart heavy with grief. The room grew cold and he was shocked to see his departed wife across the room bending over the cradle. Terrified he started muttering rapid prayers and covered his head with the blankets. When he got up the courage to look again the apparition was gone.

The next night he lifted the infant from the cradle and laid it behind him in the bed, hoping to escape the ghostly visitor if she should appear again. But he had only just put his head on the pillow once more when Grace was standing by his bed and stretching over him to wrap up her child.

'Grace dear what is it brings you back? What is it you want with me?' a shuddering Thady asked as he shrank beneath the bedcovers.

'I want nothing from you, Thady, but to put that wean back in her cradle,' replied the spectre with scorn.

'You're too afraid of your own wife but my sister Rose won't fear me. Tell her to meet me tomorrow evening in the old wallsteads.'

Rose lived with her mother about a mile away from the little cabin. As soon as the sun lighted the sky Thady ran to speak with her.

'Good God Thady Connor but you look like you've seen a ghost,' Rose greeted him.

Poor Thady's appearance wasn't helped by the fact that he hadn't slept a wink that night.

'Oh Rose, a ghost is just what I have seen,' he said. 'Your own sister came to me the last two nights.'

The colour raced from the face of Rose and she had to steady herself with a hand on the hearth. She looked about to see if her mother was there to listen and was glad to see she was in the other room.

'Whished will you,' she said and ushered him outside. 'What was it she wants?'

'She wants to meet you tonight in the old wallsteads,' he told her. 'But don't ask me to be there will you.'

Rose obeyed her sister's summons without the least fear and kept the strange tryst in due time.

'Rose dear,' Grace said as she appeared to her sister in the old wallsteads, 'my mind's uneasy about them red shawls that's in my basket. Matty Hunter and Jane Taggart paid me for them and it will be eight days on Friday. Give them the shawls tomorrow. And old Mosey McCorkell gave me the price of a wiley coat that's under the other things in the basket. And now fare-well; I can get to my rest.'

'Grace, Grace, wait a wee minute with me,' she cried as the dear voice grew fainter and her face began to fade. 'Grace darling! Thady? The children? A word.'

But neither cries nor tears could further detain the spirit from it rest.

24

THE SPIRITS OF GREENCASTLE

Earl William de Burgh was a resident in the castle at the fishing village of Greencastle. Now de Burgh had a beautiful young daughter who loved to wander about the area alone, enjoying the sights. One of her favourite places to wander was along the shore of Lough Foyle, watching the birds skim the waves with daring and elegance or the chance to spot a dolphin leaping into the air with what she imagined to be joy. She loved the sea in all its moods; on bright days when the only sound was the lapping of the waves on the shore with a gentle swish, running over the stony shore or on days when the black clouds engulfed the sky, the wind howled like a great beast and waves raged at the shore.

One day when she was out walking she got caught in a quicksand.

'Help, help,' she screamed. She had been alone on the beach and knew it was a desperate plea. But suddenly she heard a voice shout; 'Hold on, I'm coming.'

She had no idea who this voice belonged to nor did she care as the chance of rescue was close.

A young man appeared before her, throwing a rope out to her. When she saw his face she gasped, for it was that of the son of Sir Walter Burk. She knew very little of him but she knew that many of the young ladies in the area spoke of him in admiration. However, for her he was someone to avoid for he was the son of her father's enemy. But in this situation she didn't care and knew her father would appreciate what he was doing.

She grabbed the rope and the young man pulled with all his strength and freed her from certain death. She was in too much of a desperate state to notice the look on the young man's face. Yes, there was concern there but if you looked deep into his eyes there was so much more than just the feeling of concern.

'Are you ok?' the young man said. 'Here, sit on this rock to steady yourself and take my coat. You may be in shock.' He pulled a small silver flask from his hip pocket and offered it to her.

'It's brandy, it will help your shock,' he said.

'Good Sir, I am a young lady and do not drink alcohol,' she said.

'I understand that miss but you have had a shock and it is for medicinal purposes, perfectly acceptable for a lady,' he said.

She took the flask reluctantly and sipped from it.

'Oh, it is foul,' she gasped.

'I know,' he said, 'but it will help.'

'If you think it is foul why for heaven's sake do you carry it with you?' she said.

'I'm not sure,' he said, 'the flask was a gift from my father and it is the norm among young men. I'm glad I have it today.'

The young woman was also glad as despite the foul taste it had warmed her inside and settled her nerves. She surprised herself as she asked, 'Do you normally do as the other young men do?'

She was a shy young woman and rarely engaged in conversation with any young men, especially not the son of her father's enemy.

She laughed as she watched the young man's embarrassment. He laughed too and the two settled into easy conversation. They found they had much in common and the time slipped by easily.

'I must get home,' the young woman said, jumping to her feet.

'I'll see you home,' the young man said.

'No! You know that is not possible,' she said.

'But look at you, there will be questions,' he said.

'I'm fine. I'll tell them I fell down a dune. They are used to me turning up looking a little rough.' She knew she couldn't tell her father she had been rescued by the son of Burk.

'But can I see you again?' the young man asked.

'Oh, I wish we could but the dispute between our fathers prevents it,' she said gently.

'That is their business. Why should it effect our lives?'

'You know it does,' the young woman said as she walked away. She stopped and looked back at the young man.

'Thank you for saving my life,' she said, 'and it was a pleasure talking with you.'

As she walked away she knew she owed the young man her life. She had also delighted in his company. But what could she do? Go against her father? Maybe if she told him how the young man had saved her life? But she knew how her father felt about the Burks. They were allied with the O'Donnells, her father's mortal enemy.

What she didn't know was that the young man had admired her from afar for some time. He often walked the shoreline so he could watch her, hoping that somehow he could get acquainted with her. He certainly hadn't wished what had happened on anyone, especially her, but it had allowed him to become acquainted. And she was even more wonderful than he imagined. But he knew the ferocity of her father's feelings towards his own father and family. Was it possible to overcome this? Surely the fact that he had saved her life would count for something?

The young man walked the shore every day after the incident in the hope of seeing her and talking to her now that they were acquainted. But whether her father knew of what had happened and forbade her or whether she was avoiding him, he did not meet her.

Then, one stormy day, his heart leapt with joy as he watched her struggle against the wind. He tried calling to her but the words were whipped away by the wind. He made his way towards her. When he came upon her he gave her a fright as her head had been bowed against the wind.

'I'm sorry to startle you,' he said, 'I hope you are not disappointed to see me?'

'No, not at all,' she said, 'I just didn't hear you coming.'

'I've been searching for you the last days,' he said.

'Oh, father forbade me from wandering after the state I arrived home the last day,' she said. 'I don't think he believed my story. But he is away.'

The two fell into easy company again. It was clear that they were perfect for each other but how could they overcome the problem of their fathers? Neither had an answer but, with the joy that all young lovers live with, hoped that love would overcome all.

From then on they would meet in secret. The paths that they walked were deserted which meant they could walk sometimes but had to be ever vigilant.

Then war broke out between Earl William and the O'Donnell's and their allies the Burks. The two young lovers couldn't see each other under these conditions. Each pined for the other and managed to have some notes smuggled to the other at great risk to them both.

When the young man was captured Earl William showed him no mercy and had him locked in the tower to starve to death. The young woman was appalled when she heard this. She wanted to tell her father how she loved him but knew it would mean nothing. Maybe if she told him that the young man had saved her life he would show mercy?

'Father, you must show mercy to the young man in the Tower,' she said.

'How dare you! I will not show any of the Burks mercy and neither should you. They would slit your throat as quick as they would look at you. They are monsters,' he said.

'But father, the young man saved my life,' she said.

She told her father the whole story but instead of his stance softening his hatred only grew.

'I should chop his hands off for laying them on my daughter,' he roared.

'He didn't lay any hand on me father; he is a gentleman,' she said.

'A gentleman,' he bellowed. 'The Burks don't understand the word gentle or man and certainly not the two together. They are barbarians. But he'll suffer plenty as it is.'

No matter how she pleaded her father would not listen. In her desperation to save her beloved the young woman started to smuggle food to him in the tower. She was desperate to keep him alive in the hope that when the war ended they could be together, even if it meant having to elope.

Then one night she was caught bearing food to her beloved. He father was blinded by rage and hatred. He grabbed her by her long hair, dragged her to the battlements and flung her to her death. The young man heard the terrible screams and knew they were of his beloved. It wasn't long till his spirit departed in search of his love. And although the castle lies in ruin now people say that from time to time the spirits of a young man and woman can be see wandering about in search of each other.

25

THE PIPER'S TUNE

There were many people who would refer to Patsy Rogers and Dan McHugh as 'those two useless and lazy yokels'. Lazy was probably the wrong word as it didn't fully capture the lengths these two were willing to go to, to avoid any suggestion of work. But to avoid work and still have shillings in your pocket demanded a level of resourcefulness that, had it been directed elsewhere, would have made them rich. But then Patsy and Dan would say that their lives were full of riches that no money could buy.

In order to put the few shillings in their pockets the boys had taken to distilling a drop of poteen. They had found an old abandoned house up in the hills, hidden by a copse of wind-blown trees struggling to hold onto the ground. It was well out of the way and the perfect place for illicit activities.

The two lads assembled their still in the ruins of the house and set things in action. Now the lads knew more about drinking poteen than about making. They had to experiment with the process and experiment even more with the results. There were many days they were out of their heads and others where they were sick as dogs from drinking concoctions that were neither healthy nor safe – mind you, many people would say that about any poteen.

Well, whether by accident or dint of perse-
verance they hit upon the perfect mixture of
mash, the perfect length of time on the still
and the perfect, clearest drop of poteen.
They quickly bottled it up and started
looking for customers. Not that it was
hard to find customers, but they didn't
want the whole place knowing about
their activities. They went further afield
than their local area and sold the poteen.
Within a short time there was a great
demand and they had to busy themselves making more.

Now this change in fortune had a
major effect on the lads. They had plenty
of money in their pockets and even more, they were very popu-
lar. People wanted to welcome them into their homes with the
hope of getting their hands on more of the precious liquid.

All this started to go to their heads. Patsy started to dress in
fine clothes and to groom himself. He began to turn heads and
attract the eye of lots of the girls. In time he was going steady
and then shocked the whole area when he announced his intention to get married. Once he was married Patsy settled down
and stopped his wandering with Dan. But he still went with
him to the ruin to check on the poteen and business continued
to thrive.

One day they were sitting in the ruins sampling the poteen.
It was one of the finest batches they had drunk. It was a grand
evening, a lovely sunset dipping down behind the mountains,
and a good mood was on them so they sat on drinking a few
more drams.

Suddenly Patsy jumped to his feet.

'Christ, I have to be on my way,' he said. 'She'll be annoyed with me.'

'Och Patsy, you've become an awful bore since falling in love,' said Dan.

'Ah Dan it is a changed man I am thanks to the magic of the pure drop.'

'Well here's to the pure drop,' said Dan, 'and here's to your health.'

'And to yours Dan,' said Patsy. 'Are you coming then?'

'I think I'll stay on a bit and enjoy a few more thanks,' said Dan.

Dan took a bottle and sat in the open doorway looking at the sun slowly slipping from the sky. He was alone with his thoughts and the whispering of the wind.

When darkness fell around him the sound of music came to him on the whispering wind. At first he thought he was imagining it or it was the poteen playing tricks. But it kept drawing closer to the old cottage. Dan strained his eyes to see who it was that was coming but no matter how hard he tried he could see nothing. It wasn't totally dark as the moon was climbing into the sky and scattering its light about.

Dan could see no light and there was no one he knew in the area who could play music like this. It came closer and closer and crept right up to the door. Dan held his breath, waiting to see who, or indeed what, was going to step through the door-way. But as it soon as it came up to the door it started to drift away again. All Dan could do was listen to the fading tune and watch the rising moon. He thought to himself that it wasn't a tune that he knew.

Now it has to be said that Dan was not very musical. Sure he would be first to jump to his feet to dance when a tune was struck up. He would grab the nearest young woman to swirl around the floor. But he couldn't play or sing a note and would be hard-pressed to name a tune.

When the music stopped silence settled around the cottage but to his amazement the tune continued to dance in his head. Around and around it went. In a short time he fell asleep, but he awoke to the sound of the tune again but it wasn't coming from outside the cottage but from inside his head.

Dan made his way down the hill and home. Later in the day he met Patsy and up and told him about the music.

'Ay Dan, I think you had a few too many last night,' said Patsy.

'I'm telling you Patsy it was real for I feel I could play it for you.'

This brought a peal of laughter from Patsy.

'Well my friend,' said Patsy, 'let's go and find the piper and see what you can do.'

They went to the piper's house to find a large crowd gathered listening to the piper's tunes.

'Dan here has a tune for you lads,' said Patsy.

'I never took you for a music man Dan,' said the piper.

'Ah sure have you not seen him dancing to your tunes?' said one of the others.

'Oh I have but as I say, I never took him for a music man,' said the piper. That got another guffaw of laughter.

'Hum us that tune then,' said the piper.

'I can't,' said Dan, 'but I think I might be able to play it.'

This met with more laughter.

'Well I have to admire your neck Dan,' said the piper as he handed over his pipes.

Well the first notes that were driven through the pipes by Dan were terrible. But soon a tune started to flow from the pipes that brought a hush to the assembly. They watched Dan's fingers dance on the chanter with his eyes closed tight, lost in the myriad of notes. The piper watched and listened carefully.

Then the music finished and was met with silence but then the air filled with clapping.

Once he had played the tune Dan had no recollection of it and still marvelled years later when he heard it being played and people told the story of how Dan brought the tune to the piper.

26

THE WIDOW'S
DAUGHTER

There was once a poor widow woman who had a daughter named Nabla. Now Nabla grew up both idle and lazy and when she had grown to be a young woman she was both thriftless and useless. She spent her days sitting with her heels in the ashes, the cat on her lap and she crooning to it. Well, one day her mother was got so annoyed with her for refusing to work that she got a stout sallyrod and thrashed her soundly with it.

Now as her mother was giving Nabla the whacking who should be riding past but the king's son himself. He heard the commotion within, of the mother walloping and scolding and Nabla crying and pleading with her, and, reining in his horse, the prince shouted, 'What is the matter within that such ructions are pouring out?'

The widow woman stopped her thrashing and came to the door. Her face reddened when she saw who was without and she curtseyed to the prince. Not wanting to give her daughter a bad name she said to the prince, 'It is my daughter you see. She kills herself working the whole long day and refuses to rest when I ask her. The only way I stop her is to beat her.'

'What work can your daughter do?' the prince asked.

'She can spin, weave and sew, and do every work that ever a woman did,' the mother told him.

Now it so happened that twelve months before the prince had taken a notion to marry. His mother, being anxious that he should have none but the best wife, not only in Donegal, but in the whole of Ireland, had with his approval sent messengers over the whole country. They were to find the prince a woman who could perform all a woman's duty, including the three skills the widow had named – spinning, weaving and sewing. But all the candidates whom the messengers had secured were found unsatisfactory when put to trial by the queen and the prince remained unmarried. When he heard this account of Nabla from her own mother he said, 'You are not fit to have charge of such a good girl. For twelve months, through all parts of the land, a search has been made for just such a woman that she might become my wife. I'll take Nabla with me.'

While the mother was astonished, poor Nabla rejoiced at her good fortune as she saw it. The king's son helped Nabla to a seat behind him on his horse's back and saying goodbye to the widow rode off.

When he had her home the prince introduced Nabla to the queen.

'Mother, I have found the very woman that we have sought for so long but in vain, Nabla' he said.

'And tell me son, what can Nabla do?'

'All the things you named yourself,' he said, 'spin, weave and sew, and do everything else a woman should know. And moreover she is so eager to work that her mother was flaying her to within an inch of her life to make her rest when I was passing their cottage.'

'Well that sounds very promising, but she will have to pass the test,' said the queen.

The queen took Nabla to a very large room and gave her a heap of silk and a golden wheel and told her she must spin all the silk into thread in twenty-four hours. As the queen left she bolted her in.

Poor Nabla sat looking at the big heap of silk and the golden wheel in shocked amazement. And then she began to cry for she had not spun a yard of thread in her whole life. As she cried Nabla was shocked to see an old woman appear before her in the locked room. She stared at the woman's right foot that was as big as a bolster.

'What are you crying for?' asked the woman.

Nabla told her of her task.

'I'll spin the silk for you if you ask me to the wedding,' said the old woman.

'I'll do that,' said Nabla.

The old woman sat down to the wheel and started working it with her big foot. Within the shortest time the whole heap of silk was spun and she disappeared.

'That is very good,' said the queen when she came and found all the silk spun. Then she brought in a golden loom and told Nabla she must weave all the thread in twenty-four hours.

The queen left and again bolted the door. Nabla sat down and looked from the thread to the loom and the loom to the thread, wondering, for she had never thrown a shuttle in all her days. Tears sprang to her eyes and she buried her face in her hands. She sat up straight when she heard a voice ask, 'Why are you crying?'

There, standing in the locked room, was an old woman with one hand that was as big as a pot hanging at her side. Nabla told what she had to do.

'I'll weave all that for you if you'll promise me that you'll invite me to the wedding,' the old woman said.

Nabla agreed and the old woman sat to the loom. With her huge hand it was very soon that all the thread was woven into webs.

'That is very good,' said the queen when she came and found all the thread woven. And then she gave Nabla a golden needle and thimble and said that in twenty-four hours she must have all the webs made into shirts for the prince.

Again the queen bolted the door and when she had gone Nabla sat staring at the needle and thimble and looking at the webs of silk. Again she broke down, as she had never threaded a needle in her life.

As she cried a woman with a monstrously big nose appeared in the room.

'Why do you cry?' she asked Nabla.

Nabla told her of her task.

'I'll make up all those webs into shirts for the prince if you promise to invite me to the wedding.'

'I'll do that,' said Nabla, 'and a thousand welcomes.'

So the woman with the big nose, taking the needle and thread, sat down on a stool and within a short time had made all the silk into shirts and disappeared.

When the queen came a third time and found all the silk made up into shirts she was mightily pleased.

'You are the very woman for my son,' she said. 'He'll never want a housekeeper while he has you.'

Everything was made ready and Nabla and the prince were married. On the night of the wedding the couple were surrounded by a wonderful company of people. The castle was alive to the sound of joy and festivity. But as they were about to sit down to a splendid feast there was a loud knock at the door. A servant opened it and an ugly woman with one foot as big as a pot hobbled up the floor and took a seat at the table amid the loud laughter of the assembled guests. When asked which party was she, the bride or the groom's, she replied the bride's. When the prince heard this he believed that she was one of Nabla's poor friends.

The prince went up to her and asked her what had made her foot so big.

'Spinning,' she said. 'I have been at the wheel my whole life and that's what it has done for me.'

'Then by my word,' said the prince, 'my wife shall not turn a wheel while I'm here to prevent it!'

As the party settled down again another knock came to the door. A servant opened it and let in another old woman, this one with a hand as big as a stool. The weight of the hand hanging by her side made her body lean over, so she hobbled up the floor and took a seat at the table while the guests lay back, laughing and clapping their hands at the funny sight. Taking her seat the woman was asked by whose invitation was she there, to which she replied the bride's. Then the prince went up to her and inquired what had caused her hand to be so big.

'Weaving,' she said. 'I have slaved at the shuttle all my life and that's what has come on me.'

'Then by my word,' said the prince, striking the table a thundering blow, 'my wife shall never throw a shuttle again while I live to prevent it.'

A third time the company was ready to begin their feasting when there came another knock to the door. Everyone looked up and saw the servant admit an ugly old woman with the most monstrous nose you've ever seen. This woman, like the others, took her seat at the table. She was asked who had invited her – the bride or the groom? 'The bride,' she replied. Again the prince went up to this old woman and asked why her nose was so very big.

'It's with sewing,' she said. 'All my life I have been bending my head over sewing so that every drop of blood ran down into my nose, swelling it out like this.'

'By my word,' said the prince, pounding the table with such a blow that he made the dishes leap and rattle, 'my wife shall never either put a needle in cloth again or do any sort of household work while I live to prevent it.'

And the prince faithfully kept his word. He was always on the lookout to try and catch Nabla spinning, weaving or sewing, or doing any sort of work, for he thought she might at any time try to work on the sly. But Nabla never did anything to confirm his suspicions. She took her old mother to stop in the castle with her and lived happy and contented, and as lazy as the day is long ever after.

27

CROIDHE NA FÉILE

In olden times there was a man who on account of his kindness was nicknamed Croidhe na Féile. He lived with his wife in a house close to a ferry. At one time they were well-off but owing to the generosity of Croidhe na Féile they soon came down in the world. The position of the house had a lot to do with this. Whenever a storm prevented people from getting over the ferry Croidhe na Féile invited then to his home and gave them of the best that he had. Sometimes it meant keeping them for lengthy periods and as often as not he got nothing in return, but Croidhe na Féile never complained. Again and again his wife blamed him for what she called his foolishness, but he paid no heed except to tell her that she would get plenty for her day and what more did she want.

At last his stock was reduced to three sheep and there wasn't a bite of food in the house. One evening about this time a terrible storm arose and it had not much more than started when three travellers arrived at the ferry to find that they could not get across. When he saw them out there in the storm Croidhe na Féile took pity on them and asked them to stay with him until the storm had passed. They were only too glad to accept.

Croidhe na Féile went out to the field and took in the three sheep, one of which he killed for the supper. When his wife saw this she tagged and scolded but Croidhe na Féile quietly told her that she would get plenty for her day and what more did she want. The storm continued and the second sheep had to be killed and the third. One night the supper was rather scanty and Croidhe na Féile was at his wit's end to know how he would provide for the following day. But the next morning dawned calm and bright. There wasn't a ripple on the waters of the bay and the three travellers prepared to go on their way.

Before leaving the first traveller said to Croidhe na Féile, 'You have been very kind to us and I am very sorry that I cannot pay you in gold but I have here a present which might serve you better,' he said. 'It is a magic tablecloth and the moment you spread it, it will be covered with food fit for a king. Hundreds and thousands can eat from it without the supply running low.'

'Here,' said the second traveller, 'is a decanter of the best wine in the land and no matter how much is taken from it, it will always remain full. Take it and treat your friends.'

'My present,' said the third traveller, 'is not much to look at but it might come in very useful to you as you go through life. It is a rough-looking walking stick but if ever you are attacked by enemies all you will have to do is to hold it up and they will be paralysed in the track of their feet.'

Croidhe na Féile thanked them from the bottom of his heart and the travellers went on their way. Then he called his wife and without telling her anything spread the tablecloth on the old kitchen table. She could hardly believe her eyes when she saw the grand meal that was spread before them.

'Where did it all come from,' she asked, 'with not a bite under the roof?'

When she heard what the travellers had done for them she forgave Croidhe na Féile for all his 'foolishness'.

The following Sunday Croidhe na Féile invited the whole countryside to dinner.

'Anyone,' said he, 'that can see as much as the crown of my head is welcome to come.'

People from far and near came. They ate and drank to their hearts content and still there was no sign of Croidhe na Féile's store running out.

'Where is it all coming from?' people asked, but alas there was no answer.

Day after day and week after week people came crowding to the ferry, and Croidhe na Féile sent all away satisfied in everything but one, and that was where was it all coming from?

Whether it was that the story leaked out, or that people only guessed it, but the story of the magic tablecloth and decanter became known throughout the country. At last it came to the ears of the queen.

'Please send for these wonderful articles and have them brought to the royal palace,' the queen asked the king.

'Certainly not,' said the king. 'If they were kept here at the palace they would only be used to feed the rich who can well afford to provide for themselves. They are better in the hands of Croidhe na Féile, who uses them to feed the poor.'

'Well I have no argument with that but you would think that Croidhe na Féile would have sent us an invitation,' she complained.

This came to the ears of Croidhe na Féile and he immediately sent a messenger to the palace inviting the royal couple to one of his parties. They came on the appointed day and were filled with wonder when they saw the grand meal that was down before them. The greatest dinner ever cooked in the palace was only like scrapings compared to it. This made the queen more and more jealous of Croidhe na Féile. If she had these wonderful articles in her own palace she would be the most talked-about woman in the world.

She could not get this thought out of her mind and after their return home she asked the king again to send for the magic tablecloth and decanter and have them brought to the palace. But the king refused, again saying that Croidhe na Féile was making better use of them that they would make.

'Well,' said the queen, 'I am going to ask you for one other request and that is that you will give me complete charge of one regiment of soldiers.'

The king consented, little knowing what use she was going to make of them.

The following day the queen sent the soldiers to the house by the ferry with strict instructions that they were not to return without the magic tablecloth and decanter. The soldiers set out on their journey and after many days of weary walking they reached their destination. Croidhe na Féile was away from home when they arrived and there was no one to meet them but his wife. The sight of so many soldiers frightened her and as soon as they made known their business she handed over the tablecloth and decanter. The soldiers started on their journey home, overjoyed that their mission had gone so well.

They were only round the bend of the road when Croidhe na Féile returned to find his wife breaking her heart crying about the poor condition they were in. Their only means of support was taken from them and they hadn't as much as a four-footed animal in the world.

'Ah, stop your complaining,' said Croidhe na Féile. 'Did you see a lump of a stick anywhere about the house?'

'Don't be teasing me about your sticks,' said his wife, 'and the house full of them for all the good they are. It's good for you that there's nothing else to give you bother.'

After further searching Croidhe na Féile found the stick he was looking for and without saying a word about his business left the house and set out across the mountain. He arrived at the road just as the soldiers were marching up. He held up the stick which was the one given to him by one of the three strange travellers and all at once the whole regiment stopped as if they were paralysed. Croidhe na Féile went up to the general and took from him a small bag he was carrying. When he opened the bag he found it contained his tablecloth and decanter. He then lowered his stick and told the soldiers to go on their way as he had got what he wanted. He returned home and went on feeding the rich and the poor as before.

When the queen heard how Croidhe na Féile had bested her soldiers she made a vow that she would get even with him some day. Shortly afterwards, the king set out on a tour of his kingdom and was not due to be back for some weeks. This was the queen's chance and she laid her plans carefully. She sent a message to Croidhe na Féile telling him how much it grieved the king and herself that their soldiers had tried to rob him, that they had put the general to death and punished the others severely. She invited Croidhe na Féile to a dinner at the palace, saying that he was well deserving of it on account of his kindness to them when they visited the ferry.

Croidhe na Féile arrived at the palace on the appointed day and the best of everything in the land was prepared for him. The queen had it arranged with two of her officers that they were always to keep within hearing distance of herself and her guest but they were to keep out of sight unless she called for them. After dinner she took Croidhe na Féile around to the different parts of the palace, coming at last to her own bedroom. Here she threw her arms around him and before he knew what was happening she dragged him into her own bed. Still holding him she started to scream at the top of her voice. The two officers rushed in and the queen shouted to them to that Croidhe na Féile had dragged her into the bed and was guilty of bad conduct.

Croidhe na Féile was put into a dungeon and a messenger was sent off to convey the news to the king who on hearing the story went into a towering rage. He returned as fast as his horse could carry him. His sentence was that Croidhe na Féile was to be thrown into a cauldron of boiling water. The fires were set, the cauldron of water put on and everyone was holding their breath, waiting for the terrible moment.

With that a knock was heard at the palace door.

'Go and see who is there,' said the king to one of his servants. 'There are three young men standing at the door,' said the servant on his return, 'and each of them said that they have a very interesting story to tell the king and that it would be better for His majesty to hear them.'

The king was annoyed but he was also puzzled and anxious to find out what their conduct meant. He consented to hear their stories and they asked to be allowed to stand inside the door.

'Well,' said the first, 'you shall hear my story first. But I am not going to tell it myself as I don't feel like speaking much tonight. I'll ask the flagstone at the door step to take my place.'

The flagstone started moving, then began making a queer sound and at last started to talk.

'I was once a beautiful flag in the face of a cliff by the sea shore. People from all lands came and admired me and my position. Morning and evening the waves came and bathed me, and left me shining and clean. In the heat of summer fresh breezes from the sea kept me cool and in the dead of winter they melted snow from my crown. In all seasons I had spread out before me one of the most beautiful scenes created by God's own hand. But what a change has come over me since then. No one admires me now. People walk over me and clean their feet on me without giving me a single thought. I am buried in this mighty hole where I cannot see a thing but the works of man and they are seldom good works. But why am I complaining? I got a very foul do, but the lot of Croidhe na Féile is fouler still.'

Then the second visitor began to speak.

'Like my companion,' said he, 'I don't feel like talking much tonight but you'll hear the story just the same for the rigging rib will take my place.'

The rigging rib started creaking. The creaking turned into something like a lonesome wail and out of that came the talk.

'I was once a majestic tree, the pride of the king's garden. My leaves stayed green all year round. In summer seats were placed in my shadow, and I kept away the cruel rays of the sun from the greatest gentry in the world. How they admired and thanked me and when winter came I spread out my branches and protected the palace from the biting winds of the north.

'But one day the wood cutter came with axes and saws. I was cut down, cut across and rent asunder. Here I am now and no one notices me any longer. I am covered with soot, dust and cobwebs and worse still I am smothered with smoke. But where am I complaining. I got a foul do but the lot of Croidhe na Féile is fouler still'.

The king began to wonder at what the talk about Croidhe na Féile meant, but he made up his mind to hear the third story before asking.

The third traveller said, 'Like my companions I don't feel like talking much tonight but you will hear my story all the same for the queen will take my place. The queen started speaking against her will. She held her hand to her mouth to try to prevent the words coming out but it was no use. She couldn't stop herself until she had told the whole story of her treachery to Croidhe na Féile. When she had finished the king's face was as white as a ghost and there was murder in his eyes.

Everyone had forgotten about the cauldron but the fire had done its work. The king stood for a moment watching the bubbling water and then he ordered the servants to throw the queen into the depths. There was no disobeying the order and the queen herself met the terrible fate she had planned for Croidhe na Féile.

Croidhe na Féile was released immediately and returned home to continue his good work. For many years after, he and his wife lived happily at the Ferry. His wife died first and Croidhe na Féile was to the grave much later. On the day of his death the decanter split in two. The house was searched high up and low down for the tablecloth and magic stick, but from that day to this no eyes have been laid on them.

28

A QUEER STORY

In the area of Glennfinn lived Manny and Nanny Maloney. They lived a quiet life without much adventure.

One night a tramp came to the house looking for shelter. And as was the custom and generosity of the people in those times Manny and Nanny offered him shelter for the night. As the tramp filled his belly with hot food and drink they fell to chatting about nothing much. By and by Manny announced to the tramp, 'I'd be the happiest man in the world if I could dream, for I've never had a dream,' said Manny.

'And sure, what would that be worth to you?' asked the tramp.

'It would be worth the world's wealth to me,' said Manny.

'A handsome price indeed! But you do know that not all dreams are pleasant?' added the tramp.

'So I have heard but I've never had any to know,' said Manny.

'Well I think I can help you then.'

The tramp put something under Manny's pillow, told him to wear his shoes in bed and promised that he would dream that night. The tramp was shown to a bed downstairs and Manny and Nanny went to their bed.

Manny woke suddenly and remembered that he had forgotten to lock the barn. He got up and went outside. When he did he saw a light high up in the air at the end of the garden, burning on the very top of the 'fairy spink', a hundred feet up in the air.

'Well there's a sight to behold,' thought Manny. 'The fairies are having a feast tonight.'

Now Manny knew that when the fairies are having a feast they would give a person anything that they asked for and Manny decided to intrude on the wee folk. He made his way over to the hedge and could hear music and craic in full flight. Manny started to push his head through the branches so as to see the fairies and put his request to them. The branches began to prick his head amd then it suddenly turned into an all-out assault.

'Help, help, help!' Manny called, 'I'm being attacked by wild birds. Help me! They're clawing the head from me.'

'Manny, Manny, what in the name of heavens are you doing here at midnight screaming like a pig?' demanded Nanny, 'smashing down the jackdaws' nest up the chimney.'

'Oh Nanny, I don't know what's come over me,'

'Get to your bed and let us get some sleep.'

They went back to their beds and went back to sleep.

But it wasn't long till Manny shot bolt upright remembering that he forgot to give any fodder to the cows. He went out into the frosty night and began cutting what he thought was hay. His heart almost stopped when he cut off a man's head, the head of a tramp. Manny was in a bad way but he found he could stick the head back on again.

The tramp opened his eyes: 'I'm afraid I've taken my death of cold lying on this frosty night,' said he.

'Poor fellow,' said Manny. 'Come inside and I'll make you a drink of warm milk to warm you up.'

Manny built up the fire and put the milk on to heat. The tramp got in by the fire to heat himself.

'Here drink this scalding milk,' said Manny, 'and it'll make you a new man.'

The tramp drank the milk and between the heat of the fire and the hot milk, his neck began to thaw and it fell off. Manny picked it up and glued it back on. With that the tramp started to roar and woke up Nanny again.

'Musha Manny Molloy and what the dickens is the matter with you this blessed night that you're going through all these tantrums?' said Nanny. 'You've cut the head off your dog bran. Get to your bed and let me get my rest.'

Manny got the shock of his life when he heard it was his own lovely dog he had killed. He didn't know until then that Bran was a magic dog or otherwise he would not have spoken, as what he thought was a tramp that had spoken.

29

WITCH HARE

There lived a family called Hanlons near Rathmullan on the shores of Lough Swilly and across the fields in another farmhouse lived the Dohertys. Both families had good cows but the Hanlons were blessed with a Kerry cow that gave more milk and yellower butter that the others.

Grace Doherty, a young girl who was more admired than loved in the area, took a particular interest in the Kerry cow. For what reason no one could tell but one evening she appeared at Mrs Hanlon's door with the modest request, 'Will you let me milk your Moiley* cow?'

'Sure why would you want to milk wee Moiley, Grace dear?' asked Mrs Hanlon.

'Oh, just because you're so tired at the moment,' said Grace.

'Thank you kindly Grace dear, but I'm not so tired as not to do my own work. I'll no trouble you to do my work.'

In truth the Hanlons were precious about that cow and didn't want anyone going near her that might put her off in any way. Grace wasn't best pleased when she was turned away but the next evening, and the one after that, she appeared again at the cowhouse door with the same request.

At length Mrs Hanlon, not knowing how to persist in her own refusal, yielded and permitted Grace to milk the Kerry cow. But she soon had reason to regret her lack of firmness for the Moiley cow suddenly gave no milk to her owner. After this situation had continued for three days the Hanlons went to seek help from a man called Mark McCarrion who lived near Binion.

'That cow has been milked by someone with the evil eye,' he said. 'Will the cow give you a wee drop do you think? A full pint measure would do the job.'

'Oh aye Mark dear, I'll get that much from her alright,' said Mrs Hanlon.

'Well Mrs Hanlon, lock the door and get nine new pins that have never been used in clothes and put them into a saucepan with the pint of milk. Set them on the fire and let them come to the boil.'

The nine pins were soon simmering in Moiley's milk.

Soon rapid steps were heard approaching the door, followed by agitated knocks, and Grace Doherty's high-toned voice was raised in urgent entreaty.

'Let me in Mrs Hanlon,' she cried. 'Take that cruel pot off the fire! Take out them pins for they're pricking holes in my heart! Please stop it and I'll never offer to touch milk of yours again.'

Mrs Hanlon took the boiling milk off the fire and true to her word Grace O'Doherty didn't touch any milk of the Hanlons again.

Now the Hanlons were not the only ones to have problems with their milk. Across the Swilly in neighbouring Inishowen, people were complaining that their cows had stopped giving milk. They had a fair idea of what was afoot as each neighbour they told reported spotting a very large hare sitting without a care in the world staring in on the farm. Some had even taken a shot at it but it seemed to just pass right through it.

Well, one man was determined to settle this situation. One day he went out to milk his cows when he saw the hare sitting as bold as brass, looking at him. Indeed, except people said he was losing the run of himself, he would have said the hare was grinning at him.

'I have the better of you,' said the man to himself, and he went to get his gun.

As he lifted it down he had a thought; 'Now every man with a good shot has had a go at her and failed. It's more than ordinary shot I need.'

He searched his pocket and then the dresser till he found a silver sixpence.

He put it in the gun and went out to confront her. And what do you know but she sat there as if inviting him to try. He took aim, pulled the trigger, and she took off suddenly across the fields.

'Damn and blast,' cursed the farmer, as he thought he had missed her. 'I'll get you yet.'

But as he watched her go he realised that he had hit her as she was limping badly. He followed after her and took up her trail from the blood that dripped from the wound.

After about a mile he came on a neighbour's house and what did he see but the hare slipping in through the sink hole. He went to the door and knocked.

'God Bless you Tomas Doherty,' he said to the young man at the door.

'Step in,' said Tomas, 'and God bless yourself.'

When he stepped into the kitchen he saw a trail of blood through the room. He always thought Tomas was a bit of a gom and he could see that he had no notion of the blood on the floor.

'Is your mother about Tomas?' the farmer asked.

'Sure isn't she below in the bed not feeling well.'

'Well you tell your mother that next time I'll have a shilling and it will be more than "not feeling well" she'll be.'

Tomas didn't know what he was talking about but said in all innocence that he would pass on his message.

And from that day there were no more complaints about cows not milking well.

* A moiley is a cow without horns.

SALTY BUTTER

The town of Lifford in County Donegal and the town of Strabane look directly across at each other and had it not been for the river sure it would only be the one town. Indeed people moved freely between the two and businesses often operated in both. Now the imposition of the border further complicated things for the people of the two towns, as now there was an authority on both sides watching their toing and froing.

Of course it wasn't long before people started to gain enterprise out of this situation and more so when the war came. With the war came rationing. However, it affected people on the opposite sides in different ways.

For the people of Strabane butter was the thing they missed most. On the Donegal side it was tea. Now the Irish are well known for their tea drinking and the people of Donegal were wedded to the practice just like any other. It was a torture to be without it and any number of substitutes just never came close to satisfying their desires. It was known for families to scrape together a small fortune to buy a pound of tea from those who managed to have a supply.

There was one poor cratur who crossed the bridge into Strabane who had come all the way across from Gweedore.

Now she hadn't made the journey to buy anything; her interest was in selling. She had with her a load of fresh seaweed: dulse to eat and keep people healthy and kelp to use in the garden to grow a few vegetables. She called to one house with her wares and they were glad to see her. They bought some dulse. As the woman stood at the door she spied through the door the man of the house drinking from a cup.

'Ah musha there's a sight I haven't seen in many the long day,' she said.

'And what would that be?' said the woman of the house.

'A person supping on a cup of tea,' she said.

The woman in the house could see the longing on her face.

'Och sure, we have plenty of that here,' and she went and brought a cup to the woman. She watched as the Gweedore woman savoured each hot drop and smacked her lips when she finished.

'Ah God bless you daughter for your kindness.'

'You're most welcome but sure you know you could have more of that if you wanted it,' said the woman of the house.

'Och I can't be spending me few pennies on the likes of that with mouths to feed at home,' she said.

'Ah but you might not have to spend your pennies,' said the woman.

'And how is that then?' she asked, looking about with a furtive glance.

'Have you a cow back in Gweedore?'

'Aye indeed I do.'

'And do you churn a bit of butter then?'

'Ah I do.'

'Well if you can spare a pound of your butter I can spare a pound of that tea.' The woman and her husband had such a hankering for butter that couldn't be satisfied for love nor money.

'I'll be coming back next week,' she said, 'and I'll bring the butter.'

Well the week couldn't go fast enough for either family. On the appointed day the woman in Strabane set about baking a scone bread to put the butter on. But as the day wore on she thought the woman wasn't going to appear. Finally, as evening was closing in, there was a gentle knock on the door.

'God, woman, I thought you had forgotten me,' she said.

'I wanted to wait till it got a bit dark,' the Gweedore woman said, afraid she would be caught. She handed over the butter and took the tea in return.

'God's speed to you for you are a decent woman,' the Strabane women said in thanks.

The woman from Gweedore headed off towards the bridge to cross into Donegal with the tea safely deposited among her skirts.

Inside the house the family sat down with great fanfare to warm scone bread, hot tea and for the first time in months, butter. There was great excitement and chatter and a row nearly broke out over who could dip their knife into the golden block first. The father decided that they should all wait to take the first bite together.

'One, two, three,' the father counted and all five around the table tucked into their feast with gusto.

But within seconds there was a volley of shots from each of their mouths as they spat out the bread.

'Ach it tastes of seaweed,' cried the husband.

'The stupid woman must have hidden it in the seaweed,' declared the woman.

They all sat looking at the golden block of butter.

'Well we can't let it go to waste,' said the father as he picked up his bread and ate it regardless.

The others followed suit and despite one or two complaints they made the best of it.

When the woman got home to Gweedore the kettle was sitting on the fire waiting to brew up. They were soon sipping hot tea and not a hint of the taste of seaweed.

'God bless that woman in Strabane,' she declared. 'And I hope they're having as much pleasure from the bit of butter.'

Of course it wasn't just during the war that such activities were carried on. Over the years as duty and taxes varied on either side people crossed from one side to the other to purchase goods or indeed to claim benefits on both sides.

At one stage spark plugs for the car engine were half the price in Strabane than in Donegal. There was one customs man on the Lifford side who could tell by looking under the bonnet, however he did it, that the plugs came from the North. There and then they came out and you'd have to walk to get new ones locally. It wasn't long before he earned the nickname of 'Plugs'.

There was a woman who went back and forth regularly with a big old-fashioned pram. One day a smart boy stopped her and lifted the wean to discover a false bottom full of goods. Sure he thought he was the greatest thing ever. The other lads of course were never done telling him how great he was for this. Then one day she was crossing again and the lads were urging him on again. He stopped the woman and plunged his hand into the pram. But this time the woman was ready for him and his hand found itself sunk into a pile of dirty nappies.

31

FALLING OUT

There were two young lads living just outside Falcarragh who had a tragedy visited upon them in the middle of a stormy night. Their poor mother died and left them orphaned.

'What are we going to do?' said Seamie.

'Faith I don't know,' said Tommy. 'She did everything for us, cooked the meals, washed and mended our clothes and gave us comfort when we needed.'

Soon the house was a hive of activity as people arrived to wake the woman for the traditional three days and nights. Everyone sympathised with the brothers and told them how wonderful a woman their mother was. Thankfully the local women arrived too with sandwiches and scones and made enough tea to slake the thirst of an army.

The two lads bowed their heads in sorrow as she was lowered into the ground on a cold October morning. Tears welled in their eyes but each did their best to be stoic for her sake. But each wondered how they would survive without her. When they got home they sat on either side of the fire, staring at the flames.

'Sure we'll just have to manage,' said Tommy, the eldest of the two. 'Haven't we watched mammy go about her chores. We'll know what to do.'

And so they settled into a kind of routine fending for themselves; cooking, cleaning and mending. It wasn't long before the cleaning and mending went on the long finger. The cooking was a necessity as they both had massive appetites. But what they could produce themselves was never satisfactory and they argued constantly over who was the worst at the cooking.

Well they struggled through for the rest of October and well into November.

'Jayus I can't take any more of this,' said Tommy.

'More of what?' said Seamie.

'It's rock hard spuds or bags of bloody water,' said Tommy.

'Oh and I suppose that's all my fault,' said Seamie.

The two had been having goes at each other all week and this had the potential to turn into a feud.

'I'm not saying anything of the sort,' said Tommy placatingly. 'Sure one of us is as bad as the other.'

'Well what are we supposed to do then?' said Seamie.

'There's only one solution, we'll have to get a woman!'

'Ay jayus where or how are we going to get that?' asked Seamie.

Now the two had very little experience of, or indeed contact with, women. The only time they saw a woman, or spoke with one, was at Mass on a Sunday or on a Friday when they went to the post office to collect their pensions and buy a few groceries. The rest of the week they kept themselves to themselves looking after the few sheep.

'This might be the answer,' said Tommy the next Friday in the post office. He was pointing to a wee notice advertising a bus trip to Derry for Christmas shopping.

'Surely there'll be women on that,' he said.

Now neither of them had ever been beyond Letterkenny and neither of them had ever gone shopping in a big town. They walked back to their wee cottage on the back of Muckish in silence.

'Should we both go then?' asked Seamie.

'Ach there's hardly any need to go to all that bother,' said Tommy. 'We'll toss for it.'

They tossed for it and it was Seamie who got the short straw.

'Ah Tommy,' said Seamie, 'can't you go? You're older and have more experience than me.'

'Now Seamie, we said we'd toss and sure don't you cut a dash in your Sunday suit.'

Now in the village itself there lived a widow whose husband had passed away two years previously. She had gone into deep mourning, worn black, was seen in the church every day and visited his grave regularly. However, she was still a young woman and felt she had more living to do. She no longer wanted to sit at home on her beads as was expected. So despite what she thought her neighbours might say she decided to go on the bus trip to Derry.

She had her hair done in a new style and searched through her best clothes. They were a sight for sore eyes after wearing black for nearly two years. She picked out a floral blouse and a long pencil-style skirt. On the morning of the day trip she was up early readying herself. She glanced out at a blue sky and thanked God for the fine day. She looked at herself in the mirror and thought she looked wonderful. Indeed she felt great in herself. Anxious as she was she left early and was the first in the queue for the bus.

Now there was another anxious cratur heading for the bus that day too. Poor Seamie didn't sleep a wink all night and was up early to put on his Sunday best. Tommy had even gone to the expense of buying a new tie and had insisted on him taking a bath the night before even though it was a Thursday night and he had only had one at the start of the month. He could barely eat the bit of porridge for his breakfast and soon he headed off to be out of the house.

When he arrived in the village he was surprised to see the widow woman waiting for the bus.

'Good morning,' he said. 'A lovely day.'

'Oh Seamie, good morning to you,' she said. 'I didn't think this would be your sort of thing?'

Seamie didn't know what to say so he just smiled at her. Soon enough others joined the queue and a general chatter got up. Seamie and the widow fretted at the front, not sure where to look or what to say.

Thankfully it wasn't long before the bus arrived. When the door opened the widow woman rushed to get on to the bus. But as she tried to step up she was hampered by the tightness of her skirt. In desperation she put her hand back to try to open some of the buttons at the bottom and allow her to step into the bus.

Of course people in the queue were wondering what was delaying things at the front. Poor Seamie was in a sweat. Should he try to help or not? Then he put his hands to her back and shoved her onto the bus. The widow woman turned around to Seamie.

'Oh thank you Seamie,' she said. 'I was afraid that I was going to fall out there.'

'You thought you were going to fall out,' said Seamie. 'I thought I was going to fall out for it was my buttons that you were fiddling with.'

32

THE GHOST SHIP

This is a ghost story and it's true; I won't tell a lie, you know that yourselves.

Inishtrahull lies 7 miles off the Inishowen coast between Glengad Head and Malin Head and just north of Inishtrahull's Tor Rocks. And about 4 miles north of these rocks there's a small patch of fishing ground and it's only about 4 miles square. However, there's always good quality fish to be caught there. The only problem is, there is a permutation of factors which must be in place before you can fish there.

Of all places that I have fished this is the loneliest, darkest and most dangerous spot I've ever had the misfortune to fish on and a requirement to fish here is that it must be dark, tides must be slack, it must be flat calm, and finally you don't go there if you're tired or sleepy. The patch of ground is in the middle of dozens of old shipwrecks, which is why it is named 'Tullyally' after the car breaker's yard in Derry.

I was steaming home after fishing on Downings Bay and Lough Swilly for a couple of days, when I got as far as Dunaff Head. I realised I wasn't going to get to Greencastle in time to catch the lorry for Dublin, so there was no rush. I had twenty-four hours till the next lorry. A slight alteration of course would take me to Tullyally and conditions were perfect for such an adventure. So this is what I did.

We shut away the net and started to tow in the usual way. Normally you'd tow for four hours. We were towing for three hours and it was now three o'clock in the morning. The rest of the crew was asleep as was normal. Suddenly a large ship appeared, steering straight at me out of nowhere. This was an old type of ship which was out of circulation for years, what I would call an old three island tramp ship. Although I remember I had my hand on the throttle I made no effort to reduce speed. There was no sound and she came so close that I could see a man standing aft on the docking bridge. He was wearing a dark overcoat and a peaked cap. He never moved and just stood with his hands on the railings. The two vessels came together in a head-on collision, bu there was no sound of breaking timber or any damage. The ship actually sailed through my boat. I saw the man go right through my fore-mast. She sailed on in the direction of Malin Head and it just faded away.

At no time was I in any way frightened but I just called the crew and hauled in the gear. I never mentioned my experience to the crew as I thought they wouldn't believe me. Or if they did believe, they would not want to come here again, so I just kept my mouth shut.

We had a good bag of fish and in among the fish was an old rotted blue jumper and a peaked cap. I may add here that on this patch of ground that was quite normal as it was in the middle of shipwrecks. However, at the same time I feel I disturbed someone's grave.

What was the meaning of it all?

From then on when I did go back to Tullyally I always avoided the exact spot where I had encountered the ship.

However, many years later I was talking to a man, much older than me, who also fished this ground. He asked me if I had ever experienced anything unusual on that ground and I told him I did. He was about to tell me something but other people joined us and he just said we would talk again sometime. He died shortly after and I am still wondering if he had the same experience. I will never know.

I earned my living from the sea for forty years and in all that time I've never had a similar experience like that. Also I'm very sceptical of stories like that, and I usually take them with a pinch of salt. So if anyone reading this feels like taking a pinch of salt I'll understand because I am the only person who knows that it is true.

ACKNOWLEDGEMENTS

I remember asking the much-missed storyteller Shiela Quigley where she got a story from. Her reply was along the lines of 'here and there, floating about in the air'. The essence of being a storyteller is being a good listener, always alert to new stories and catching those wisps floating in the air. Some of these stories have come to me in this way, snippets heard here and gathered there, requiring further searching. Others came in fuller detail and were then shaped and moulded to my own telling. My thanks to all those people, whatever the age, who have shared snippets with me over the years.

My thanks to all at the History Press and particularly Beth Amphlett for her patience and understanding.

My thanks also to the following people for their help in following up material and helping to put this collection together: John Quigley, John McGlinchey, The Staff at Central Library Letterkenny, Áine McKenna, Mary Montgomery, Eddie O'Kane of Cavanacor Gallery, Donegal Fiddler Martin McGinley, Storyteller Liz Weir, Charlie McCann and Criostoir MacCarthaigh at the Irish Folklore Commission.

Some of the stories are taken from collections and are acknowledged below:

Balor of the Evil Eye: This version differs from the more established version from the Mythological Cycle. I first became familiar with it from the Faoil in Falcarragh. This version is to be found in *The Annals of the Kingdom of Ireland by the Four Masters*, collected by the translator John O'Donovan from Shane Dugan of Tory Island.

Paddy the Piper: This was collected by Samuel Lover and published in *Legends and Tales of Ireland*.

Jamie Friel and the Young Lady: I first heard this story of from my friend and mentor Liz Weir and it was collected by W.B. Yates. Far Darrig in Donegal, Grace Connor – A Ghost Story and Bewitched Butter were also collected by him and were all originally published in *Fairy and Folk Tales of the Irish Peasantry* in 1888.

Rats on Tory: I first heard this story on RTE Radio 1's Mooney Goes Wild programme. A man rang in to explain why there are no rats on Tory Island and told this story. A short time later I was telling stories at Cresslough Day Care Center as part of Bealtaine Festival. I was introducing the story when one of the men identified himself as the person who told the story. It was lovely to meet   Bill Gallagher who insisted on me telling the story. Afterwards we had a great chat. He introduced me to the rich heritage that surrounds St Colmcille and gave me a prayer card with the two clays mentioned in the stories. Sadly he passed away a few years ago but it is lovely to keep his memory alive with this story.

The Widow's Daughter and The Old Hag of the Forest: These were collected by Seamus MacManus and first published in *In Chimney Corners, Merry Tales of Irish Folk Lore*, 1899.

The Bee, The Harp, The Mouse and The Bum-clock: This appeared in *Donegal Fairy Stories*, first published by McClure, Phillips & Co. in 1900.

The Glenties Midwife: This was collected by Elizabeth Andrews and published in *Ulster Folklore*, which is available on The Project Guttenburg.

The Eagle's Nest and The Legend of Raithlin O'Byrne: These were taken from *The Cliff Scenery of South West Donegal* by Kinnfaela.

A Queer Story: Taken from the Schools Collection of the Folklore commission and used with kind permission of the Irish Folklore Commission. Collected by Bernard Doherty, Goland, Ballybofey, Co. Donegal, from his grandmother Mrs A. Flanagan, Cappry, Ballybofey, Co. Donegal, aged 65 years. IFCS 251: 191-194.

Croidhe na Féile: Taken from the Schools Collection of the Folklore commission and used with kind permission of the Irish Folklore Commission. Collected by Pádraig Mac a Goill, Árd a Raí, Co. Dún na nGall, from Dómnaill Uí Breisleain, Corr, Leitir Mic a'Báird, aged 65 years. IFCS 243: 119-128.

Falling Out: This story came out of a wee yarn in the book *Old Time Jokes and Story* by Paddy O'Grady and is used with kind permission.

The Ghost Ship: This story was collected from Jimmy Doherty whom I met through An Grianán Theatre's 'Sense of Memory Project' and used with his kind permission. It is also published in 'Shared memories of Derry and Donegal' by Serenity House Creative Writing Group.